# Death comes to Strandvig

## Diane Hansen-Ingram

To Helene and Vibeke, my fellow winter Bathing Belles.
*Fordi vi har kun det sjov vi selv laver!*

To the Flylady system for helping me get rid of the clutter in my house, and – more importantly – the clutter between my ears.

To my Mum, who loves a good cozy. And to my dearly-departed-Dad, who would have loved the food at Strandhøj Kro.

With thanks to Kathryn for being a listening ear
and having a good eye.

With love to KRE.

# RESIDENTS OF STRANDVIG

*Jannick Andersen:* Trainee Assistant, Æblegården Nursery

*Bent Bang:* Retired, member of the Viking Swimmers Club

*"Holy" Helle Brandt:* Chairperson of the Viking Swimmers Club,
Cantor at Strandvig Church
*Hans Jørgen Brandt:* Her husband

*Martin Brix:* PR Executive
*Maria Brix:* His wife
*Mathias Brix:* Son, kindergartener at Æblegården nursery
*Mathilde Brix:* Daughter, kindergartener at Æblegården nursery

*Daniel Bro:* Incident Commander, Strandvig Police

*Bertil Bruun:* Bike dealer
*Anne Bruun:* His wife

*Gustav Damborg:* High school student, Dish washer at Strandhøj Kro
*Mette Damborg:* His mother
*Lærke Damborg:* His sister

*Kenneth Frandsen:* Proprietor, Frandsen Brothers store
*Henrik Frandsen:* His partner

*Karsten Holm:* Proprietor, Strandhøj Kro
*Lisbeth Holm:* His wife

*Johnny Højer:* Barman at Strandhøj Kro

*Lea Jensen:* Admin Assistant at Strandvig Council, member of the
Viking Swimmers Club

*Gerda Larsen:* Retired, member of the Viking Swimmers Club

*Elvira Lund*: Retired, Secretary of the Viking Swimmers Club
*Ida Lund*: High school student, Waitress at Strandhøj Kro

*Margit Meyer*: Cleaning lady, Strandvig Police Station

*Ellen Møller*: Widow, Butcher
*Brian Møller*: Son, Driver
*Morten Møller*: Son, Accountant
*Jacob Møller*: Son, Butcher's Assistant

*Ole Olsen*: Retired, member of the Viking Swimmers Club
*Yrsa Olsen*: His wife

*Karin Rasmussen*: Leader, Æblegården Nursery
*Stig Rasmussen*: Handyman, Strandhøj Kro

*Mads Sørensen*: Unemployed, former member of the Viking Swimmers Club

*Sonja Thomsen*: Nursery Assistant, Æblegården Nursery

# DANISH – ENGLISH GLOSSARY

I hope the use of Danish will be apparent from the context. But here is a small glossary for reference.

The Danish alphabet consists of 29 letters: the letters æ, ø and å appear after z.

*Ama'r halshug!*: Cross my heart and hope to die

*Den dumme skid*: That bloody idiot!

*Far*: Father or dad

*Farvel*: Goodbye

*For fanden*: Bloody hell

*Gammel Dansk*: Danish dram

*Godmorgen* : Good morning

*Hygge*: Cosiness, warmth

*Hyggelig*: Cosy, warm

*Kro*: Inn or Tavern

*Kroner*: "crown", Danish unit of currency

*Pyt*: Never mind

*Skat*: Darling, dear

*Skål!*: Cheers!

*Vi ses i morgen*: See you tomorrow

*Æblegården*: Apple orchard

*Øv!*: Oh no!

WINTERBATHING GUIDELINES


Winterbathing Guidelines issued by
the Danish Council for Greater Water Safety
*(Rådet for Større Badesikkerhed)*


## BEFORE YOU GO IN THE WATER

1. Never swim alone
2. Check bathing conditions and identify rescue equipment
3. Beware of ice on stairs and bridges
4. Lower body calmly into the water


## WHEN YOU ARE IN THE WATER

5. Breathe slowly
6. Keep an eye on each other
7. Stay close to stairs and stairways
8. Never swim under the ice

CHAPTER 1

8 January

*I must be mad!* Lea Jensen forced herself not to shiver as she removed her heavy, blue bathrobe, placed it in the wire basket and looked down at the wooden steps, sparkling with thick frost. Focus, Lea! She put one hand on each side of the railing and descended slowly, feeling each step with her bare foot to check for ice. At the last step she sank slowly into the water, looked straight out to the horizon and kicked off. She counted: one stroke, two strokes, three strokes… At four, the sea won, the icy water biting into her neck like tiny steel blades. She turned full circle and thrashed back to the steps as fast as her basic breaststroke would carry her. Grabbed on to the thick, wooden rope that was circling in the water like a snake, and pulled herself up on to the first step. She was panting, the air from her mouth blowing out in little clouds of steam.

"*Godmorgen,* Lea Mus!" She looked up to see Bent Bang, her friend and senior Viking, grinning down at her. His smile only slightly larger than the somewhat ragged blue towel loosely hanging round his waist.

"And a very good – and very frosty – morning to you, too, Bent!" Lea reached the top of the steps and allowed Bent to help her into her robe. He held it out majestically, as high as he could, but Lea still had to bend backwards slightly to reach down to his height. "Ah, luxury – my very own butler!" She stood up to her full height and shook her shoulders.

1

"Anything for you, Princess!" said Bent, saluting. Lea slipped into her fur-lined crocs, and looked down at her feet with a sigh.

"Princess, Bent? In these ugly crocs I'm more like one of the ugly sisters! Honestly, when did I turn into such an old maid?"

"You're not an old maid, Lea Mus. You just need to get out more and enjoy yourself. Let it all hang out!"

She rolled her eyes. "'Let it all hang out?' Just like you, you mean?" Lea pulled the robe tightly around her and felt the inner warmth that always followed an icy dip begin to surge around her body, starting with her toes.

Behind them came the sound of chattering voices. Elvira and Gerda, two ladies in their late 70s, slowly made their way across the glistening wooden boards, hanging on to each other, in a kind of soft-shoe shuffle. Like two elderly Bambis on ice. On finally reaching the railing, they carefully started to disrobe.

Bent made a flourish with his hand, as if he was removing a top hat. "Good morning, young ladies! I do hope you'll both be joining me in the sauna afterwards?"

"Of course!" tittered Elvira. Then, trying her best to look innocent, added, "Though it looks like standing room only in there this morning."

"Don't you worry, my dear", winked Bent, "there's plenty of space on my lap!"

"Oh my word! Is that a threat or a promise, Bent Bang?" quipped Elvira.

"A promise, my dear!" Bent pulled his hand across his neck, as if he was slitting his throat. "*Ama'r halshug!*"

Elvira did her best to look coy and held up her little hand towel in front of her nose. Gerda did her best to look suitably shocked. Then both of them giggled and they continued down the bathing bridge steps, chattering like schoolgirls.

Lea tried her best to shoot him a reproving look, "Bent, you're incorrigible! And," she added, nodding down at Bent's waist, "talking of 'letting it all hang out'… Are you quite sure that towel meets our club guidelines? I'm pretty sure that Frandsen Brothers have some nice fluffy towels on sale right now."

Bent looked at his towel, confused. Then looked at his towel again. "What on earth do you mean, Lea Mus?"

Lea pointed over towards the club's noticeboard, hanging in the little alcove between the ladies and gents changing huts. A piece of shiny, laminated A4-paper stuck out like a beacon amidst the hotchpotch of faded photos, and yellowed documents.

"Right there, Bent. Congratulations, you've just made the front page!"

### VIKINGS
*Male bathers are respectfully reminded that*
*their vital parts must be covered at all times*
*with an adequately sized towel.*
### H. BRANDT, CHAIRPERSON

Bent craned his neck and peered up at the paper, then down at his waist, "*Hov, hov!* What's wrong with the size of my towel? Though, I can assure you that there's nothing wrong with my vital parts, Lea Mus. All present and correct and in working order!" He turned around and looked back in the direction of the bathing steps. "Just you ask Gerda. Or Elvira!"

Lea laughed, "Oh, Bent, you're the giddy limit! But, hey, you'd better look sharp, 'cos here comes Holy Helle right now!"

Helle Brandt, or "Holy" when she wasn't within earshot, Chairperson of the Viking Swimmers Club, was striding towards them, resplendent in her winter uniform of floor-length real fur coat and matching Davy Crockett furry headband. "Lord, Bless us all! I'm off. See you tonight, Lea Mus!" whispered Bent, and darted towards the gents changing hut. The constant damp made the door stick so he pulled hard, using both hands. Luckily for him, it gave way on the first attempt this morning.

Helle Brandt was a woman with a mission. For the past three years she had devoted her time and (seemingly boundless) energy to her two 'callings': as the iron-fisted Chairperson of The Vikings and as the booming, officious Cantor of Strandvig Church. An arrangement fully supported by her loyal husband, Hans Jørgen. He was overjoyed when Helle landed the cushy, public servant post of Cantor. Not only did it bring in a very tidy sum of Danish *kroner* every month, but all those extracurricular weddings and funerals kept her permanently on her feet. And out of his hair. Which meant more time on the golf course for him. Halleluja!

Helle waved majestically at Elvira and Gerda, who were up out of the water and leisurely making their way back across the glistening boards, and headed straight for Lea.

"Good morning, Lea! Morning ablutions well underway? No better way to start the day is there?"

"Yes—" Lea started to speak, but Helle was in full flow and obviously working her way through the day's agenda. Check, check, check. And double check.

"Was that Mr Bang I saw just now?"

"Yes, he—"

"I declare he disappears like a rabbit! Oh dear, oh dear, I really wanted a word with him."

"Well, if you like I can—"

Helle started to pull off her gloves. "He promised to fix the door of the storage hut last week and it's still jamming. Did you hear that Mrs Møller got stuck in there yesterday morning – most unfortunate!"

Lea rubbed her hands together and tried to cut the conversation short. "Ellen Møller? That's a shame. Well, I had better get moving—"

Helle wasn't listening. "Luckily one of the other Vikings heard her knocking and graciously came to her rescue. But, of course, we Vikings are always ready to help those less fortunate…"

4

Lea, starting to shiver, had had enough of being cut off. "Helle, I'm heading for the sauna. If I see Bent, I'll make sure to give him your message."

Helle cocked her head to one side. "Will you? Oh, many thanks, Lea. A sense of community is so important, don't you think? And do sign up if you can lend a hand with the Moonlight Bathe next week."

Helle said this lightly, as if it was a request. But after years of experience, Lea knew better. It was a direct order. A Holy Decree. Helle fixed Lea in her gaze. "Just a tray of cupcakes. No need to go to any bother."

Lea stood in silence, determined not to engage Helle in any way. She would not bake cupcakes. She would not bake cupcakes. No, she would not. This time she would stand her ground. She was busy at the office right now and she would not allow herself to be walked over by Helle. Or anyone else for that matter. She could make her own decisions. She was a big girl, wasn't she? It had to stop. This year things were going to be different. It would be her New Year's resolution. She would not—

Holy Helle thundered on. "You will? Oh, great, thank you, Lea. I knew we could rely on you and we do need all hands on deck!" She pointed down at the wooden boards. "Hands. Deck! Ha ha ha!"

Lea, dazed and stunned, tried to blurt out a protest, but all that came out was, "Ha?"

Helle pulled back her thick fur sleeve and checked her watch. "Well, I must be on my way, Lea – you mustn't keep me here chitchatting with you all morning, however pleasant that may be. Yes, I wish I had time to bake. But some of us are busy, busy, busy, you know. We can't keep the mothers and tots waiting for Baby Psalm Song Time now, can we?" she bellowed, and marched off.

No, we can't, thought Lea, sending daggers into Helle's rather buxom disappearing back, along with a few choice (and less than holy) expletives.

5

Lea saved a few expletives for herself, having once again failed to stand her ground. Gah! From now on, she would stand firm. This year she would be...immovable. Then promptly decided she had better get moving into the sauna in order to defrost her fingers and toes.

# CHAPTER 2

Strandhøj seaside hotel, with its white-washed walls and shiny black wooden pillars, was the very last building on the coastal road out of the village. Built back in 1896, it had undergone extensive upgrades over the years. Nothing drastic in the structural department – the layout and the rooms were very much the same as they were over a hundred years ago. But the interior walls had been stripped and repainted several times. And always (always) according to the original colour charts. When the wallpaper had to be replaced, an architect from Copenhagen was brought in to track down a suitable substitute, with the remit of keeping as close to the original pattern and style as possible. After much humming and hawing by the architect, and many weeks of searching, rolls of substitute paper were found. Fit for a Queen and cost a King's ransom.

And then there were the electrics. Strandhøj had been rewired from top to bottom to conform to the ever-increasing safety standards and (more importantly) the ever-increasing desire of guests to be online twenty-four hours a day. High speed internet, please, and make it snappy. The indoor climate was just as important, so draughty single pane windows had been replaced by low energy double glazing. And, more for pleasure, all the bathrooms had been equipped with underfloor heating. But despite the modern improvements, the grand hotel had managed to retain all of its old world charm. The wooden staircase and 'herring bone' pattern wooden floors were in a league of their own. Regularly and lovingly maintained by a local family firm of joiners – the same firm who had installed them in 1896 – they were a thing of beauty. The first thing one noticed on opening the main glass doors, entering the small reception.

So Strandhøj remained proudly (though never snobbishly) true to its original style. Over a hundred years and a couple of decades since it's opening, there was a decidedly chic, genteel feel about the place.

There was something decidedly less chic and genteel about Johnny Højer as he pushed the overflowing trolley full of white satin-weave bedding and white damask tablecloths to the car park. Johnny's hair was, at the best of times, what can only be described as 'wild'. Despite his best efforts to tame it. On this cold and frosty morning, it was downright flat on one side and bolt upright on the other. And he looked like he'd much rather be lying down inside the trolley rather than pushing it from the outside.

The white laundry van came Tuesdays, Thursdays and Sundays. It was already parked at the back door of the hotel with its doors wide open, the faintest sound of pop music coming from the front. Brian Møller, the driver, hummed along with Dodo and the Dodos. He loved this radio station: all his favourites, all day long. His musical taste hadn't evolved since his teenage years, and he was quite content with that. Brian was in his standard winter uniform of grey shell jacket and grey thermal trousers. If you replaced his woollen hat with a helmet, he wouldn't have looked out of place on the slopes of the French Alps.

Johnny let out a yawn, patted his hair down and rubbed his hands together. Damn, it was cold! "Hey there, Brian! Good morning!"

Brian, busy unloading black felt doormats and the day's batch of fresh linens from the van, turn around and stopped. "Oh, hi there, Johnny! Where's Stig this morning? Sick?"

"Nah, we swapped shifts. One of the radiators at *Æblegården* isn't working, so Stig's taking a look. You know him, Mr Goody Two Shoes. Want one?" Johnny, shivering, held out a packet of Prince, took one himself and lit up for both of them.

Brian took a puff. "Thanks, Johnny. *Æblegården*? So he's off helping Karin then?"

Johnny sat down on the wall, using one of the dirty tablecloths to protect his backside from the cold stone. "Yeah. Not a bad looking woman, Karin. Got her own flat too – all very nice and stable. A man could do worse."

Brian laughed, "Sounds like you might be interested in the little lady yourself, Johnny?"

"Might be." He inhaled deeply and made a few smoke rings. "Like to keep my options open though. You know me, Brian, I'm a mover and a shaker. Talking of which," he said, stubbing out his cigarette on the wall and throwing it into the bush behind, "I've got some gear I need shifted. You interested in driving?"

Brian was immediately on the alert and took an unconscious half-step back. "What kind of stuff? Nothing dodgy, is it?" Brian, bless his little heart, was an easy-going guy and would be the first in line to help a friend in need. He spent all his free time coaching Strandvig's Under 7s football team. And a very good coach he was too. Firm but fair. Just like his mother, Ellen, the town butcher. But using the company van after hours was very definitely outside his comfort zone. And Johnny wasn't a friend. Or someone that Mrs Brian at home would approve of…

Johnny looked towards the hotel and lit up another Prince. "Oh, don't worry, Brian. Nothing dodgy. Just don't have a big enough van that's all."

Brian gently shut the back doors of the van, making as little noise as possible. "What about Stig, is he in on it?" Stig was a different kettle of fish, he'd done Brian plenty of favours in the past. And Mrs Brian approved of Stig, there was no doubt about that.

Johnny screwed up his eyes and took a long drag. "If you're not interested, Brian, it's okay. I'm sure I can find another driver. But, hey, have a think and let me know as soon as possible, will you?" He smiled and rubbed his fingers together. "Because there might be a good bit of money in it for us."

9

CHAPTER 3

Gustav Damborg slammed the door behind him and
started running down the three flights of stairs. He
was holding on to his very scuffed, dirty green Fjällräven rucksack
with one hand and trying to pull on his North Face parka with the
other. When he got down to the bottom of the stairwell, he stopped
and half turned. First he patted his pocket, then started to fish in his
inside right pocket. The bike key wasn't there. Shit!

He started to reclimb the stairs, two at a time, but changed
his mind at the first landing and knelt down, panting slightly. He
opened the bag and pulled out his laptop. Then turned the bag
upside down and shook out the rest of the contents onto the
linoleum... Come on, come on, it had to be in there somewhere!
Gustav was going to be late for gymnasium. Again.

Several scraps of A4-paper, various plastic folders, three
dog-eared textbooks, an empty packet of cinnamon rolls, two plastic
coke bottles (one with a lid missing), the remnants of a broken
plastic triangular ruler, and various pens and pencils. All inkless. All
pointless.

Gustav spied the familiar round figure of Eric Cartman
amongst the rubble – the keyring had been a Christmas gift from his
little sister. He put it between his teeth and started to pile things
back into the rucksack. But lying on top the rubble of his belongings
was a little crumpled packet.

He looked around the stairwell. Not that there was anybody
about at that time in the morning. His Mum had left for work an
hour ago, his little sister leaving just afterwards to walk to school.
And the two old biddies who lived on the first and second floors

didn't make any noise in the morning until their carers had been in to help them wash and dress. After that, the TVs would blare all day, but right now there was total silence. And then it all went pitch black. Total darkness.

He stood up and felt around for the stair light switch. It clicked and the light returned, together with its tick-tick-tick sound. He grabbed the packet from the floor. Mum! If she ever found out... Gustav was not only tired and late, he could now top it all off with a very large helping of guilty conscience. He stuffed the packet into his top parka pocket and zipped it up. And scooped the rest of the jumble back into his rucksack, stuffing it down and flipping over the top. There was no time to worry about Mum right now. And anyway, it would be over soon.

Outside in the courtyard, the grass was white. Gustav could feel his ears and the tip of his nose starting to tingle. Not just tingle – they were actually beginning to burn from the cold. What was it – minus 15 this morning? And he had absolutely no idea where his gloves or hat might be. He checked his pockets, well knowing that he had just emptied them in an attempt to find his bike key. He'd been at Strandhøj last night – had he left them there? Then again, they might be in his room. They could be anywhere in his room. He looked up at the windows from the courtyard and then at his watch. There was no time to go back and look. He could hear Mum's voice in his head:

*"Have you seen my gloves, Mum?"*

*"No. Have you tried your room? Though you'll be lucky to find anything – it looks like a bomb has gone off in there..."*

*"Never mind, I don't need them, it's fine."*

*"When did you last have them on?"*

*"Mum, if I knew that, I wouldn't be looking for them now, would I?"*

*"Did you have them on when you cycled back last night?"*

*"I told you, Mum, I can't remember!"*

*"You'd forget your head if it wasn't screwed on——"*

*"It doesn't matter. I don't need them anyway!"*

*"But it's cold out there and—"*

His bike glistened. A few drops of condensation dripped off the tyres. Great, it was shaping up to be a fantastic ten-minute bike ride. Nothing better than plonking your bum on an ice-cold bike seat. He used the sleeve of his parka to rub off the worst of the frost. And to think he actually laughed when Mum had wanted to buy him a lambswool cover! The guilt came flooding back.

He pushed the packet to the back of his mind. Oh well, not all was rotten in the state of Gustav's world. At least there was something in his day to look forward to – tonight at the Kro. Gustav had checked the hotel work schedule twice (for the record, he had checked it three times, just to be sure) and he and Ida would be working the same shift. He was the dish washer at the Kro. She had been promoted to serving. And they would battle together, in the kitchen, with their playlists. Ida was a Lukas Graham girl, he was into The Minds of 99 but they could always meet over Kashmir.

A tingling sensation went right through his body, and this time it wasn't due to the sub-zero temperatures. He hadn't been sure at first – I mean, Ida was friendly and polite to everyone, wasn't she – but the last couple of times she had looked at him, it had seemed liked she really liked him. *'Liked him'* kind of liked him. Gustav had been trying out one of the flirting tips he'd seen in his little sister's tween magazine. God forbid Lærke should ever find out that he had been reading it and tell her schoolmates. He would be the laughing stock. On the other hand, Lærke's friends were always giggling when he was around. Girls!

It had sounded stupid when he had read it in the magazine, but he was getting desperate and decided to try it out. Staring at Ida when she wasn't looking, then turning away when she looked at him. Several times in a row. And last night when he had done it, when she had come in with the huge stack of plates from the Old Boys' Badminton table, she had held his gaze for just a little bit longer and seemed to blush. Though that might have been because she had been run off her feet: those Old Boys were a handful. But, no, he was sure that he wasn't imagining things. Maybe tonight he should make his move? He was wearing his lucky underpants... Yes, he'd ask her tonight.

Gustav managed a small smile and bent over and unlocked his bike. Adjusted his earbuds, pulled the sleeves of his coat as far down as possible over his numbed fingers and walked out of the courtyard, walking a little bit taller with every step. He got out into the street, took a deep breath and put his leg over the crossbar. It was then that he noticed his gears were frozen. Brilliant, just bloody brilliant.

# CHAPTER 4

Karin Rasmussen switched on the kettle and looked out the window. She loved icy January mornings – the frost made the tops of the playhouses shine as if they were covered with diamonds. Soon they'd be covered with wriggling, toddler bottoms.

"Cup of coffee, Stig?"

"Yes, thanks, love. I'll just nip out and get my toolbox."

Karin had arrived at *Æblegården* nursery at 6.30 am, as she always did on Thursdays. Jannick opened on Mondays, Sonja took Tuesdays and Wednesdays. Karin unlocked the main gate and the front door. Switched on the table lamps in Red Room and Blue Room and started on the day's bread dough. She loved the repetitive morning ritual of mixing and kneading in complete silence – the calm before the storm. She moved the large bowl of dough to one side and took two white Ikea mugs out of the overhead cupboard. A spoonful of Nescafé for each, splash of milk for her, plus two sugars for Stig. He really didn't need a biscuit with that amount of sugar in his tea, did he? But she liked to spoil him.

Stig was lying on the floor of the laundry room, tinkering with the radiator underneath the changing table. She stood with his cup and a blue plastic bowl piled high with biscuits.

"Think you can fix it?"

"Yeah. Just needed a new valve. Should be finished in a couple of minutes."

Stig and Karin had always been together. They met in the school playground, were best friends through school, dated through gymnasium and moved in together as soon as they had enough

14

money to leave their respective Strandvig nests. And so it had continued until they both turned 30, and the world expected them to act like adults. The pressure was on to buy a house: their own place. And they slowly realised that, in truth, they would each prefer to have a place of their own. It would be wrong to say that things had dried up because there had never been strong flowing currents of passion in the first place. Their love for each other was more of a babbling brook. So there was no big bust up, no pay-outs and no fights over kids: children had never been part of their equation. Karin and Stig were comfortable with each other. Filing for divorce had never been an option, quite simply because it had never crossed their mutual mind.

"Done! Should be warm in about 10 or 15 minutes." Stig warmed his hands on the cup and took a couple of biscuits from the plastic bowl. "Anything else need fixing?"

Karin smiled, "Round here? There's always something that needs fixed! Actually Jannick said to me last night that one of the lamps at the back of the carport isn't working. But I'm not sure if we have any of those special bulbs left. You'll need to take a look in the shed."

"Okay," said Stig, taking another biscuit, "will do."

"Only if you have time, though. It's not urgent." Karin looked at her watch, "Hey, shouldn't you be up at Strandhøj?"

"Nah, it's okay, Johnny said he'd open up this morning. You know, Johnny. Always keen to lend a hand. Could have been a boy scout!"

"Boy scout, my elbow. Johnny only helps out if there's something in it for him, you mean. Always looking for the next big break. Or easy money. He'll end up getting his fingers burnt one of these days…"

Stig decided that it was best to say nothing and continued to munch on a biscuit. He had heard it all before from Karin and nothing he could say would change her mind. Once she'd made her mind up about someone, she wouldn't budge. And when it came to

15

Johnny, he really couldn't blame her. He'd known Johnny for as long as he had known Karin, because all three had gone to school together. Johnny and Stig in one class, Karin in the year below. The boys in Stig's class played football together at break and lunchtime. After school the whole pack would head into the forest to build dens. Stig's favourite time of year was the autumn, when they'd collect hundreds and hundreds of chestnuts and lie on the grass listening to the red deer bellowing. In the summer months the boys would bike down to the beach and skim stones. And they always ended up swimming, more often than not, in their underpants. They had been good times.

Stig had looked up to Johnny. He was the unspoken leader of the pack, the one who dared do things that the others only dreamed of. The one who was forever getting in trouble, or forever getting others into trouble. Most of the kids were in awe of him and quite a few were scared of him, which meant that he was never short of an audience. Stig wasn't quite so comfortable watching Johnny in action. Like the summer afternoon when the pair had gone into the petrol station on the coast to buy ice-cream. Stig could only look on dumbfounded as Johnny – very deftly – stole two packets of cigarettes while the attendant was busy operating the noisy metal soft serve ice-cream machine. Stig felt dreadful, not having had the courage to stop Johnny, especially as the attendant was a teenager they both knew from Strandvig.

*"Why did you do that, Johnny? That was Mikkel's big brother!"*

*"Relax! No-one saw us. Here you go, one packet for me and one packet for you. We're in this together."*

*Stig had put his hands in his pockets and looked down at the ground.*

*"I don't want the cigarettes! You stole them, you keep them."*

*"OK, scaredy cat, I will. If you don't want them, I'll give them to Mads."*

*"But what about Mikkel's brother. He'll see that there are packets missing!"*

*"I said 'relax'! The petrol station makes plenty of money..."*

16

*"But what if Mikkel's brother has to pay for it?"*

*"Shut it, okay, Stig? God, you're such a goody two shoes…"*

They had eaten their ice-creams in silence and Stig was glad to finally be able to bike home to the security of his mum and dad. Though he was just as shocked as they were when he opened his satchel later that night and a crumpled packet of cigarettes, still in its squeaky cellophane, fell out.

Stig had burst into tears and the whole story came out. He was scared of Johnny, but he was even more scared of his parents' reaction. From that moment, Stig's parents made him cut the connection. He'd gone to bed that night, sobbing, trying to stifle the sound with his pillow. His mum had come in, sat down on the side of the bed and rocked him to sleep, just like she had done when he was a toddler. For Stig it had been a relief to end the friendship and, kudos to him, Johnny hadn't minded in the least – "No sweat, Stig, I've got plenty of other mates". And now, twenty years on, here they were, back together here in Strandvig. Workmates who looked out for each other.

"…and I really wish you'd stay away from him!" Yes, Karin was on a roll.

"Well, working at the Kro together, there's not much I can do about that, is there, love? Besides, it was him who offered to cover for me this morning, so it's really thanks to him that you now have a fully functioning radiator!"

Stig felt it again. The heat was slowly coming back, but the air in the room was very definitely glacial due to Karin's silence. "Johnny's alright, love. Just give him a chance." He held Karin's face in his hands and gave her a big peck on the cheek, "He just needs the love of a good woman, that's all. We can't all be that lucky!"

Karin tried to scold him. "Oh, you big, soppy thing. Run along with you!"

Stig picked up his tools and threw the packaging from the valve into the bin. When he turned around, he found Karin emptying the bowl of biscuits into one of the drawers in his toolbox.

"Oi! Are you trying to fatten me up?"

"Don't want you wasting away, do we now?"

"Oh I get it. You don't want all the other girls running after me..."

Karin pretended to hit him on the arm. "Just you behave yourself!"

Stig picked up his toolbox and blew her a kiss, "Don't I always, love? Oh, by the way, did you hear who's back in town?"

"No."

"I'll give you three guesses!"

"Stig, I haven't got time for this, the kids are arriving. Just tell me!"

"Mads."

"Are you sure?"

"Yes, met him down at the Kayak Club – he's back for good."

"Oh."

Karin waved Stig off and went back into the kitchen. Mads was back in Strandvig? She hadn't seen that coming at all. She could hear small voices in the corridor: time to get cracking.

# CHAPTER 5

Martin Brix, in his dark blue Swedish slim-cut suit and dark brown leather shoes, stretched across the back seat and strapped Mathilde and Mathias into their car seats. They sat up straight, like little dolls, in matching pale blue and pale pink all-in-one ski suits. Matching pale blue and pink balaclavas, matching pale blue and pink gloves. And matching grey camouflage Angulus boots. Everyone could see they were twins, so why the blazes did Maria insist on dressing them alike?

He stood upright and shivered slightly, patting the pastel, striped, cashmere scarf around his neck, as if it would somehow magically transfer heat to the rest of his body. He daren't adjust the scarf because it had taken him a full five minutes in front of the mirror trying to make it look like he had – nonchalantly – just thrown it on.

Still, it was better not to say anything to Maria – anything that would spark off yet another argument. Thank God he had another late meeting at the office tonight – the perfect excuse to stay on for dinner in Copenhagen. He'd heard so much buzz about that new seafood diner in *Kødbyen*, the old Meat Packing district, just a few minutes' walk from his company's loft offices. But Martin had a small niggle at the back of his head. What was that old saying about eating shellfish…to avoid eating it in the months that contained the letter R. Or was it the ones that didn't? He dismissed the thought just as quickly as it had popped into his head. Two of his co-partners in the advertising agency (therefore, Martin's 'rivals') ate there last week, so he had better go there tonight. It was dog eat dog in this business. Or fish eat fish. R or no R.

19

Martin sat down carefully behind the wheel and clicked the remote to open the electric garage door. He ran his hands over the steering wheel while he waited for the door to lift open, put the BMW into gear and gently rolled the car out of the dark garage into the blazing, white light outside.

A toddler's voice piped up from the back seat, whisking him back from the cool, hip Meat Packing district to the cool, icy tree-lined street.

"But is she?"

"Is she what?"

"Mum? Is she picking us up. Mum?" Mathias knew that dad took them to nursery and mum picked them up.

"No, I'm afraid not. Mum won't be finished until late today."

"*Neeeeeeeeeeeeej!*" chorused Mathias and Mathilde.

"Ida is coming to pick you up—"

"*Jaaaaaaaaaaaaaaa!*" chorused Mathias and Mathilde.

Ida, a girl who went to the local high school, was their favourite babysitter. The twins had encountered numerous babysitters in their short toddler lives, but Ida was, to date, the only babysitter who hadn't quit after a week and wasn't fazed by Mother Maria's impossibly rigorous standards. Maria demanded stability and consistency for her children, but Maria herself was capricious and consideration for others didn't figure in her calculations. Ida didn't seem to mind the endless changes of plan at the Brix household: being summoned at short notice or being dropped at the very last minute. Saint Ida was, moreover, hugely popular with the children. She let Mathias and Mathilde eat ryebread with *chokolade pålæg* (thin slices of chocolate) as an afternoon snack – eating rather a lot of slices herself – if they promised to eat a piece of ryebread with *leverpostej* (liver pâté) first. Ida was also good at reading stories and also a dab hand at building Duplo. A star in anyone's book.

"Will she make us pancakes for dinner?"

"No."

"*Øv!*" chorused Mathias and Mathilde, greatly displeased.

Silence from the back seat.

"She's just going to bring you home and play with you until Mum gets back."

"But she makes better food than Mum!"

Martin had to agree on that one, but chose to ignore the remark. Who could blame the kids for turning up their noses at a solid diet of spelt and quinoa? Never mind celeriac burgers parading as the real thing. His own suggestion of local, organic beef burgers having been shot down like a big fat duck. Yes, now that he thought about it, he was pretty sure that it was the months containing R that were safe. He blinked his eyes. He'd enjoy some lobster tonight. Perhaps a small steak to follow. No sauce. Just lean protein.

Still silence from the back seat.

"Ida's working at the restaurant tonight, so she can't stay for dinner, even if she wanted to." Martin had never been a fan of Strandhøj. He considered it too 'local' for his taste. The food was good, but the clientele? Well, he'd never say it out loud, but to him they were 'provincial'.

Ida, on the other hand, he admired. She had spark and a lot of potential. So why was she wasting her talents up at Strandhøj? Her smiling face popped into his head. Oh, yes, she was very pretty too. He blinked his eyes and made a mental note to pursue that. Hadn't he just recently overheard her mentioning a gap year to Maria? Their current office girl would soon be leaving them and Ida would make a great replacement. Yes, he'd ask her tonight. Strike while the iron is hot. Martin's personal motto. He didn't let opportunities slip through his fingers. His raised his right hand and swept the hair back behind his ear.

Martin edged the BMW slowly down the ramp towards the street and waited for a couple of bikes to pass. He checked himself in the rear-view mirror and ran his hand over his cheek and jaw. He'd exfoliated this morning and had used both primer and moisturiser. He was pleased with what he saw, and settled his back

21

into the heated seat. The car turned silently out into the quiet street, heading left along the coast towards *Æblegården* nursery. It should only take four or five minutes, even with this morning's hard frost on the roads. Though there was a perfectly good clock on the dashboard, Martin constantly checked the Rolex on his arm. The sight of it, between his crisp white shirt cuff and his tanned hand pleased him. Yes, they'd be there in plenty of time. Maria would have his guts for garters if they arrived after the 9 am watershed.

Continuing silence from the back seat. Mathias and Mathilde had been well taught by their mother. It was some small consolation to him that at least they didn't pout. Not yet. But that day would surely come.

"Hey, it's Thursday, *tur dag*. Do you kids know where you're off to today?"

"The beach!" shouted Mathias. Unable to keep up the silent treatment any longer.

"Are you sure, Mathias? In this weather?" Martin shivered inwardly and looked out his left window at the pavement which had been white with ice since Christmas. He was definitely not the nature-loving, outdoorsy type, unless it involved skiing on the French slopes or dining alfresco with clients. For him, being outside didn't involve any kind of action as such, but more the fact of being seen. In the right light and circumstances. With the right people – preferably the young, tanned and lovely kind. And wearing the right clothes, of course.

"Yes, *far*! We're going to collect branches, there are lots of them down at the beach. Because Jannick, you know Jannick? He's nice, he plays football with me and Victor. And he's really good at drawing dragons." Mathias turned to Mathilde and tried to scare her. "Roarrrrrrrrrrr!" Mathilde looked at him blankly and hugged her small, white fluffy rabbit even closer to her.

"Do you like dragons, *far*? But Jannick's really good at building castles, too. Isn't he, Mathilde? I think castles are cool. But I like football better. So does Victor. Well, Jannick said that if we get enough branches we'll make a bonfire in the playground this afternoon."

"Uh huh." Martin had far more important things on his mind at this very instant. Like where he should buy his morning coffee. His usual fix was a skinny double shot latte from the tiny café near his office. But that could entail a potentially treacherous walk on icy pavements. He also spared a loving thought for his leather shoes and decided that, no, he would play it safe and stop at a petrol station on the way.

"And Karin said, if we get enough branches, and if Jannick makes a bonfire, she'll make us a giant bowl of dough. And you know what you can do with the dough, *far*?"

"Hmm?" He was still weighing the pros and cons. The petrol station didn't do juice shots. No, he'd go to the bar. Nadja knew his usual order and, what's more, Nadja knew immediately the second Martin came through the door whether he had time to linger. Whether she should chat or leave him alone with his headset. He appreciated the little details like that – that was great customer service. Nadja's smiling face popped up in his head. He blinked his eyes, the decision was made. He would start the day with a power vitamin shot. It would be a long day, after all.

"Make *snobrød*! Yum! And then we'll have bonfire bread for our afternoon snack. Isn't that right, Mathilde?"

Mathilde, suddenly brought back to life, nodded. She lifted up fluffy Ninka Rabbit and pressed her against her cold nose. And glowed. *Snobrød*! She couldn't think of anything better than *snobrød*. Well, perhaps *snobrød* dipped in strawberry jam.

CHAPTER 6

Bent Bang, having successfully avoided Holy Helle, finished dressing. Every day – rain, wind or shine, Easter or Christmas – started exactly the same way. He cycled down to the Vikings on his old Raleigh. Dip, sauna, dip. Followed by a cup of coffee with the Oldies. Just the way he liked it. The Oldies were a small hard-core group of bathers – many of them founding members of the Vikings – with a longstanding, unwritten agreement to meet on the bathing deck every morning. Or at least every other morning. They had foolishly thought that retirement would give them more time: in fact, most of them were kept busy by constant requests from their children to babysit grandchildren. So every other morning it was.

The men supplied a bottle of *Gammel Dansk* or Bitter and the ladies took it in turns to bring a thermos of coffee. In the spring, summer and autumn they sat out on the old wooden benches on the deck, looking out to sea. In the dark, dark, depths of winter they enjoyed their wee nip and black coffee in the anteroom to the sauna.

Unlike the majority of their elderly counterparts, the Oldies seemed to age slower. Something they loved to point out to each other, but never bragged about to outsiders. Their body parts didn't – as they had all feared – droop and head south at such an alarming rate as the rest of the population. Indeed, the longer they bathed, the more their sense of humour and lust for life seemed to increase. The ladies were convinced that their taut, youthful skin and cheery disposition was all down to winter bathing. "Yes, my dears," as Bent took great delight in pointing out, "we're just like in that film "Cocoon", except that our secret is cold Danish sea water!" Other theories were put forward. That being naked before God ("…and each other!" as Bent also took great delight in pointing out) was a humbling and restorative experience for the mind and soul. That the salt, iodine and natural minerals in the seawater had moisturizing, healing and revitalizing effects on the skin. But in the end most of the male Oldies were downright certain that their sprightly condition was all down to one thing: enjoying a wee dram every morning. *Skål!*

Bent pulled on his old grey overcoat and bright yellow woollen beanie hat. The same he wore every day of winter. In summer he didn't wear a coat, and swapped out his woollen beanie for an army green cap. He carefully rolled up the little blue towel, stuck it under his arm and started his goodbyes. Shook hands with the gents and kissed the ladies goodbye. Which, given Bent's fondness for his flock (or "harem" as Lea liked to call it) could take quite some time.

He said his parting *adieu* and looked up towards the entrance gate, making quite sure the coast was clear. It had been a near miss earlier. Bent made a mental note to get the first round of drinks in tonight to thank Lea – even though it always pained him to bring his wallet out in full view – she really was a star. Her quick thinking had saved him, once again, from the clutches of Holy Helle. Why did that darn woman have to act like a sergeant major? He'd used this towel for twenty years and never had any complaints! And he said he would fix the door.

He neared the clubhouse gate. There was no need to be running around after him every five minutes with a big stick. For Pete's sake, they were all volunteers. Would serve Mrs Bloody High and Mighty right if she got stuck in there herself! Bent laughed to himself at the image of Holy Helle stuck behind bars, rattling them to get out. Bent sighed and took out his bundle of keys. He thought for a second, was about to walk through the gate, then turned back around. Gah!

The image of Holy Helle stuck behind bars had morphed into a new one: Ellen Møller, panting and out of breath, sitting on a damp bench waiting for her breath to return before she tried calling out for help again. Bent felt more than a pang of guilt. He walked slowly back towards the bathing bridge, then round the back of the sauna towards the storage hut. The old toolbox should still be in there. No-one else ever touched it. Except Ole. When it was last used was anyone's guess.

There was a sound behind him and he stopped to look over his shoulder. But there was no-one there. The only eyes watching him were the seagulls, sitting in a row on the wooden railing and even they looked bored this morning. All puffed up and trying their best to keep warm. He turned back around and started turning over the keys with his weather-beaten fingers. Here was the one he needed.

## CHAPTER 7

Strandvig had a comfortable feel about it. It was undoubtedly sleepy but certainly not 'lived in'. There was definitely more emphasis on *chic* than shabby. Which was mainly due to its geographical position in the Whisky Belt: the area north of Copenhagen where the residents can, despite the best efforts of the Danish income tax authorities, still afford to drink the stuff. If you walked down Strandvig's main street, you had a good chance of meeting someone you knew. "Or run the risk of meeting!" as crotchety old Bertil Bruun, the bicycle dealer, always took great delight in pointing out.

There were all the usual chainstores you'd expect to find in a small Danish town. *Matas,* the drugstore. *Fætter BR,* the toy shop. *Bog og Idé,* the bookseller. One fairly pricey, ergo fairly well assorted supermarket, *Irma.* One fairly cheap, ergo basic supermarket, *Netto.* Plus, a decent array of locally-owned clothes and speciality food stores.

Despite years of restructuring (read: cutbacks) to the national train network, Strandvig could still boast a local station with two departures every hour (on the very civilised, hour and half hour) to the Danish capital, Copenhagen, just twenty minutes away. But, even with the big city within easy striking distance, the *Strandvigere* (the local natives) were faithful to their village and supported their local stores. Without the baker, butcher and bike shop, Strandvig as they knew it would die out and end like all the other ghost towns in the outskirts of Denmark. The local community was strong. They all pulled together. "And bathed naked together!" as Bent Bang always took great delight in pointing out.

Bang in the middle of Strandvig high street was "*Brdr. Frandsen*". Frandsen Brothers was one of those shops you often find in small towns. Part gift shop, part purveyor of soft furnishings, candles and decorative items. Though the atmosphere '*chez* Frandsen' was *bijou* rather than provincial homely. And the gifts were very definitely 'fine' as opposed to those in the pocket money category. The Frandsen Brothers provided service with a knowing smile. All purchases were stylishly and lovingly wrapped by Kenneth, while Henrik brought you up to date with all the local gossip.

To be perfectly frank, the name hanging from the wrought ironwork sign was misleading. Kenneth Frandsen and Henrik weren't blood brothers. Or brothers of any kind at all. But the kitsch couple had been living together for so many years, and were such an integral part of life in Strandvig, that their nickname had stuck. Indeed, most *Strandvigere* couldn't remember Henrik's real surname. Henrik seemed to have completely forgotten it himself. It was happily tucked away somewhere at the very back of his memory. Very conveniently right along with his birth certificate, which was happily tucked away somewhere at the very back of a very deep drawer that was very permanently locked shut.

At 9.45 am precisely, Kenneth Frandsen unlocked the front door of the shop. He looked out into the street. It was just starting to get busy again at this time of the morning. Rush hour was an hour and a half ago, and the clothes and speciality stores opened their doors at 10 am. Only the supermarkets opened earlier. He called out a cheery '*godmorgen!*' to Jacob, one of their regular customers, who was whizzing past on a bike. Kenneth breathed in and shivered – another icy morning – but beautifully sunny. Something to add to his happiness journal tonight! He hated the long, dark Danish winter days. They put him into a long, downward spin and made him yearn to climb further into his shell. December was a fairly easy month to get through, with a constant daily focus on the *hygge* of Christmas and the hustle and bustle in the shop. But January could be grey, foggy, cold and damp. He revelled in the current weather of snow

28

and ice. As much as he despised the cold, the snow made everything white and bright. Yes, he was a child of light! Kenneth took a deep inward breath and turned his face upwards, in an attempt to soak up every single ray of sunshine.

He continued to hold the door open with his foot and smiled approvingly, while Henrik carried out a couple of large grey wicker baskets and placed them on each side of the small, but perfectly (mis)formed, rustic wooden bench outside the shop. Kenneth released his foot and followed suit, scurrying out with deerskins in hand. He ceremoniously placed them on the bench and finished his rather grandiose *tableau* by lighting candles in several enormous black metal French lanterns with a long stainless steel candle lighter. *Voilà!* His job was done! *Så hyggelig!*

Meanwhile, Henrik, his better (and very much larger) half, was back inside the warmth of the shop, lighting fragranced candles, which were dotted around the displays and in the windows. His last task before opening was watering succulents. Frandsen Brothers didn't sell flowers as such, but there was constant demand for their array of small plants, which were just the right size to sit on a narrow window ledge or on a bathroom shelf. And both brothers enjoyed seeing the pale green foliage – it made for a soothing background in the shop. Right along with the soft tones emanating from the shop sound system. Henrik and Kenneth alternated between two CDs – the Best of Classical Music and the Best of Lisa Nilsson. Henrik and Kenneth weren't true pop or jazz fans but their favourite diva sung in Swedish, and that made it much more palatable. And rather classy.

The gleaming steel Italian coffee machine gurgled happily in the background. Henrik's eyes flashed to the Georg Jensen clock on the wall: a couple of minutes before 10 am and they were ready. Just like clockwork. Henrik reached for a huge glass mason jar that was on the right of the till, unscrewed the lid and gazed inside: *Kongen af Danmark*. Ruby red lozenges which, if you believed the story (and Henrik saw no reason not to) had been eaten by Danes since the seventeenth century, taking their name from King Christian the

Fifth. Henrik wasn't a huge history buff but, having a keen eye for detail and a sharp memory for the unusual, remembered that one of Christian's favourite pastimes, according to the King's own memoirs, was love-making. Hunting, maritime affairs and war weren't quite so noteworthy, going with the turf.

According to legend, King Christian – when not busy wooing – suffered from a sore throat. But despised the cure of the period: aniseed oil. The King's physician, not to be outdone, came up with the bright idea of mixing the bitter tasting oil with a sugar mass in order to mask the taste. King Christian enjoyed the resulting product and, *voilà*, Denmark's favourite cough drop was born. King Christian was cured. But died after a hunting accident in 1699, at the age of fifty-three, having fathered eight children with his wife and six with his mistress.

Fifty-three. Henrik winced. He returned his gaze to the mason jar in front of him then slowly and deeply inhaled – letting the bitter aniseed aroma reach his nostrils – then daintily put in his chubby forefinger and thumb, selected a red jewel, taking great care not to touch the others, slowly extracted it from the mason jar, looked at the crown stamped on the sweet, then ceremoniously popped the boiled sweet into his mouth. *Gud bevare Danmark!* God bless Denmark! The observant bystander would also spot that Henrik's eyes briefly flashed over to the opposite wall, where 'Daisy', the current reigning Danish monarch, Margrethe the Second, sat very majestically in a beautiful silver frame, looking down with pride upon the shop floor. Henrik pondered whether Daisy ever enjoyed a King of Denmark?

Kenneth took small, noiseless sips of his espresso and sat down at the counter with his phone. He peered through his reading glasses and checked his messages, muttering out loud with the occasional "aha" or "hmm". The last message gave him pause for thought. He sat motionless and shifted his eyes to the side, trying to determine whether Henrik was behind him. Kenneth read the message twice, saving it word by word to his internal memory, then pressed 'delete'. He switched off his phone and placed it without a sound on the shelf underneath the counter.

He lifted up his cup, not realising that he had already drained the last of the espresso, but he completed the action anyway. Then replaced the cup on the saucer, making a little too much noise and disturbing the stillness in the shop. He cleared his through and coughed. "Um, Henrik?"

"Yes, *skat*?"

"How about eating up at Strandhøj tonight?"

"Of course, *skat*, whatever makes you happy!" Henrik, still sucking the sweet, had started to fluff up the sheepskin cushions that were stacked together in neat piles on top of a black lacquered bench. "Any particular reason?"

Kenneth swallowed hard, "Um, no, Henrik. No particular reason…"

Henrik turned away and started refolding a pile of Klippan lambswool rugs. Then suddenly stopped and pointed an accusing, chubby finger at Kenneth. "Wait a minute… I know what you're up to!"

Kenneth felt a shiver running down his back. And this time it had nothing to do with the sub-zero temperature outside.

"It's Thursday, right? Little Friday! Ok, hold on a minute…" Henrik picked up a pile of glossy magazines from the top of a set of antique, French nesting tables and looked underneath for the local paper, '*Kystbladet*'. It was a large, broadsheet-style newspaper but only a few pages long. Too thin, as if the second, third and fourth sections of the newspaper had somehow been lost along the way. *Kystbladet* reported the news from the towns up and down the coast but, as there really wasn't much local news to report, it was mainly filled with adverts, 'offers of the week' from Strandvig's two competing supermarkets and the ubiquitous (and, all too often, self-written, glowing) portraits of local citizens turning 60, 70, 80 or 90. Or celebrating 25 years working at the local bank. Plus the mandatory weekly death notice. Henrik spread *Kystbladet* out on the counter and opened it at page 3, his very favourite page. The 'Where 2 Eat' section. Though Henrik still referred to it as the "Dining Out" page, not in the least impressed by the snazzy name change made when two local schoolchildren had spent a week's work experience at the newspaper offices last spring. Henrik liked kids but had an aversion to kidz.

"Dum, de, dum, de dum...", he ran his finger down the page. "Here we are! Strandhøj Kro." A large smile came over his face. "Oh, Kenneth, I knew you were up to something!"

Kenneth swallowed hard and his stomach flip-flopped. His hand went straight to his phone and he pushed it further underneath the counter, right to the very back.

"You've been ever so fidgety today!"

"Have I?" Kenneth consciously put his hands on the counter and his feet on the floor and told them to stick there. Trying all the while to breathe normally.

Henrik unconsciously patted his stomach, "It's *stegt flæsk* at Strandhøj tonight. Am I right? I am, aren't I?"

"Yes. Yes, that's it."

Henrik came over and squeezed his arm. "Ha ha, you can't fool me!"

"No!" Kenneth squirmed. "No, of course not, *skat*. I wouldn't dream of it..."

CHAPTER 8

Karin checked the clock in the kitchen – 4 pm – and switched off the lights. She popped her head around the door of Red Room.

"That's me off, Jannick! Bye kids, see you all tomorrow!"

"*Farvel*, Karin! *Vi ses i morgen!*" the kids chorused.

"Right you are, Karin!" Jannick was on the floor of Red Room, surrounded by four girls who were battling over plastic dinosaurs and a Play Mobil pirate ship. Jannick himself was putting the finishing touches on a very strange looking edifice made out of Lego. Mathilde, Ninka Rabbit in her lap, was sitting beside him, looking on in wonder. And looking very angelic despite a very large smudge of strawberry jam on her left cheek. The smudge itself contained bits of black fuzz, no doubt from repeated close contact with Ninka Rabbit's nose. Jannick leant back. "Ta da, Mathilde – we're done! One fairy-princess-cowboy-fort."

Karin popped her head back round the door. "And don't forget about the towels in the dryer, will you? Perhaps Sonja can hang them up before she leaves. No, forget that, she's in the playground, I'll tell her myself when I go past."

Jannick looked up. "Roger that! Oh, and I'll make sure that Filippa gets an extra snack. It's getting late isn't it?" He didn't need to look at his watch, most of the children were collected at the end of afternoon snack time.

"Oh, thanks, Jannick, you're a sweetheart! I left an extra roll for her in the breadbin. See you in the morning!"

Mathilde's gaze immediately switched from the fairy-princess-cowboy-fort to Jannick. She prodded him with her pinkie and looked up at him with her huge brown eyes. "Can I have a roll?"

"Mathilde, you already ate at least three rolls at the bonfire this afternoon. And you've still got jam on your nose!"

Mathilde wasn't easily put off. "I didn't eat them all myself. I shared them with Ninka Rabbit. And poor Ninka Rabbit is still hungry and it's the only thing she likes…" She held up the rabbit with both hands and stuck it into Jannick's face.

He laughed. "I'm really sorry, Ninka Rabbit, but we don't have any left. Besides, you should be eating carrots and hay. Not rolls and strawberry jam. I'm sure you've got lots of them at home."

Mathilde giggled. "Yes! But I want a roll. And jam!"

"No can do, Mr Bunny. Tell you what—"

Mathilde giggled. "Ninka's a girl! Look, she's got a princess crown."

"Oops, very sorry, your Majesty." Jannick looked very grave. He pointed at the Lego-fairy-princess-cowboy-fort. "Tell you what, Ninka Rabbit—"

Mathilde shoogled the rabbit in his face again. "Princess Ninka!"

"Okay then, Princess Ninka. How would you like to be the Queen, I mean Princess, of this very special fairy-princess-cowboy-fort."

"Okay…" Mathilde didn't look convinced. "But I'm still hungry…"

A voice came from the door. "What, are you hungry again, Mathilde?"

"Ida!" Mathilde ran over to the new arrival, and threw her arms up and around Ida's waist, then buried her head into Ida's vintage fur coat. Jannick clumsily got to his feet, looking slightly embarrassed and held out his hand.

"Er, hey there – you must be Mathilde and Mathias' babysitter?"

Ida rocked to and fro with Mathilde attached to her, smiling. "Yes, I'm Ida." She sniffed and looked down. "Hmmm, you smell of smoke, Mathilde. And you've got jam on your cheek." She took Mathilde's face in her hands, and peered closely. "By the looks of it, I'd say strawberry." Mathilde beamed. "So putting two and two together, I'm guessing you've been eating *snobrød* out in the playground today?"

"Spot on, Sherlock!" Jannick loved to channel Sherlock himself. And, on catching his reflection in a mirror on a rare good hair day, liked to think that he shared more than a passing resemblance to Benedict Cumberbatch.

Ida smiled. "Elementary, my dear Watson."

Mathilde loosened her grip on Ida's waist and held up Ninka. "His name's not Watson, it's Jannick." She turned around reprovingly. "And naughty Jannick won't let Ninka have a roll!"

"Well, Jannick is perfectly right. Ninka will get a carrot as soon as we get home. And you, young miss, can get a nice piece of ryebread with liver pâte—"

"And *chokolade pålæg*!"

"Yes, okay, chocolate too if you eat the liver pâté first. You know the rules. Now, where's Mathias?"

"Out in the playground with Sonja and the other kids."

"Oh, right. Didn't see him on my way in, but it's already dark out there. And cold!" Ida shivered.

Jannick stepped forward, moved T-Rex into his left hand and held out his right hand to Ida. "Nice to meet you, by the way."

Ida, who was now battling with Mathilde – who was currently scaling Ida's back like a mountain climber – managed to free her own hand to return his greeting. "So you're the famous Jannick who can draw cool dragons?"

"At your service."

"Mathias talks about you all the time. When he's not talking about football, of course." Ida managed to shake Ida off. "Well, we must get going. Don't want Ninka to get hungry now do we?"

"It's Princess Ninka today", added Jannick, winking.

Mathilde ran over to Jannick, took his hand and started dragging him over towards Ida, "I want you two to get married!"

Ida laughed and then made a sad face. "Sorry, Mathilde. But I haven't got time for that today." She looked up. "Besides, I'm sure Jannick is already married. What with him being so cool at drawing and building," she looked over at the Lego, "erm, things."

"No, he's not! He doesn't even have a girlfriend!"

Jannick looked on awkwardly then knelt down in front of Mathilde. "Hey, I thought you and me were going to get married, Mathilde?"

"Don't be silly, Jannick! I'm going to marry Ninka Rabbit! Or Daddy." She turned around and grabbed hold of Ida's coat. "So you can marry Ida!"

Ida winked at Jannick. "Maybe another time, right? But, hey, cool t-shirt!"

"M.M.M. Have you heard of them?" Jannick wasn't used to anyone taking particular note of what he was wearing. Especially not here at the nursery, where the feature most parents recognised about Jannick was a new pair of eyes, ears and hands to look after their child. They really wouldn't care less if he arrived at work wearing a top hat, a fez or a feather boa around his neck. Which, in point of fact, could be the case at the end of the working day if he allowed the kids from Red Room to dress him using their favourite items from the dressing up box. Which he often did. So the fact that someone noticed his work attire was unusual. And the fact that someone recognised the name of the underground band emblazoned on that particular t-shirt was downright unheard of.

"Muzzy Meets Millie? Sure! I saw them when they played at Roskilde Festival last year."

This day just got stranger and stranger. Jannick was beginning to think that he had fallen down Princess Ninka's rabbit hole.

36

Ida lowered her voice slightly. "Not that I really remember it well. The Apollo stage, right? About 1 am?"

"Ha ha, yeah! I don't remember much about that night myself. I was very drunk." The words were out before Jannick heard them himself. Why did he say that? And it wasn't even true – he only ever drank a couple of beers at most. God, he must sound really stupid.

Mathilde – bored by what was obviously turning into grown-up talk, and the attention turning away from herself – took Ida's hand and led her towards the door. "Ninka's hungry. Let's go!"

"Yes, sorry Jannick, we should get going. I'm taking the kids home and then I've got a shift tonight up at Strandhøj. It was nice to meet you. See you around!" She picked up Ida into her arms. "Okay, let's go find Mathias!"

"Oh, okay. Yes, see you around, Ida!" Jannick waved to them as they left the room. He turned back around to find the four remaining girls still at war: the plastic dinosaurs were putting up a brave fight, but seemed to be a poor match for the cutthroat Play Mobil pirates. He decided to let them battle it out on their own while he put the Lego back in the toy box. Well, Ida seemed nice. And Roskilde too. Yeah, really nice. And she worked up at the Kro? That's funny, he had never seen her in there, or had he? Maybe he should—

He was knocked out of his reverie by a Play Mobil pirate ship sailing precariously close to his curly-haired, landlubber head.

## CHAPTER 9

The hotel's inn, Krostuen, was packed to the gunnels tonight. "If it isn't the oldest swinger in town!" shouted Karsten, as Bent and Lea squeezed in through the doorway, trying not to let too much of the warm air escape out into the street.

"The usual, Bent, a small draft beer?"

"Don't mind if I do, Karsten. Yes, *en lille fadøl* for me." He glanced at Lea, as she struggled in with her large handbag. The bag was stuffed full and looked like it might erupt at any minute. "Oh, and a glass of white for Lea Mus here".

Karsten Holm, owner and proprietor of Strandhøj Hotel, took a full step backwards. "Opening up your wallet tonight, Bent? Well, well, well. What's the big occasion? Won the lottery, have we?" Karsten put the glass of white wine on the bar then did a fit of ducking and diving, swatting his huge hands above him. "Damn moths! Must have come out of Bent's wallet. Probably haven't seen the light of day in years—"

Bent chuckled. "You know what I always say, Karsten… Yes, it's true, I may be stingy with my money. But I am always very, very generous with my body!"

Lea screwed up her eyes. "Eew, Bent, please – you're putting me off my dinner!" She looked up at Karsten. "So what's on the menu, *Mein Host*?"

"Tonight it's a cracker!" Karsten looked around. "You can always tell when it's *stegt flæsk med persillesovs* on the menu. The whole town is here!"

Fried strips of pork belly served with boiled potatoes and white sauce flecked with parsley was, admittedly, not the most attractive sounding dish. But it was hearty, belly-filling food – one of the Danish classics – and any self-respecting inn would serve it up "*Ad libitum*". The Danes, unable to resist unlimited amounts of pork or indeed, pork of any description, came out in force when it appeared on the menu. And tonight the residents of Strandvig were doing just that.

"You can say that again," said Lea, pulling off her thermal gloves and unravelling her long grey scarf, which was wound round her neck three times, "the car park is almost full and I had difficulty finding a place to put my bike." Lea did her best to squash her gloves and scarf into the already bulging handbag, but gave up and put them on the back of her barstool. She eagerly took her glass of white wine from Karsten. She was flushed from her bike ride and the heat inside Strandhøj was intense.

Lea lifted her glass towards Bent, and then Karsten. "*Skål*."

"*Skål*, Lea Mus!" Bent looked around, "Manning the decks yourself, Karsten?"

"No, Johnny's here – he's in the cellar changing a barrel. Lisbeth and Ida will be run off their feet with it being *stegt flæsk* tonight, so Stig's staying on to help until the kitchen closes."

"All hands on deck, then?" said Lea. And immediately heard Holy Helle's voice in her head. No, I refuse to bake bloody cupcakes!

"Yeah. Mette's lad, Gustav, is supposed to be along here too tonight according to the duty roster, but you know teenagers." He sneezed. "That was half an hour ago and there's still no sign of the young rascal!"

"Don't worry, Karsten. I've just seen young Gustav," said Bent, "I saw him talking to Stig in the car park when we came in. Or rather, Stig was talking to him. Reading him the riot act."

"Good, because Gustav really needs to pull his socks up. I let him come and do a few hours here and there because I felt sorry for him when his dad left. It was Stig's idea. He and Karin have

39

looked out for Gustav since he was at nursery. But now he's a bit of a liability, you know. Only turns up when it suits him."

"Oh, give him a chance, Karsten. He's just a boy." Lea took a sip of her wine. Listen to her, talking like an old granny!

Karsten sneezed again. "A lazy teenager, you mean."

"Oh, Karsten", said Lea, "were you never young and foolish yourself? Just take a look at our Bent, here. He never grew up!" She winked at Bent, who winked back and lifted his glass to her.

"*Skål* to that, Lea Mus!"

Karsten nodded, "Oh, here we go. Here comes the lad now." Stig had just entered the bar, followed by a sullen-looking Gustav. Gustav headed straight past the bar without looking up. "Hi Gustav, so glad you could finally join us. Get that parka off and your apron on. And look sharp about it, eh? The dishes are piling up in there."

Gustav scowled and slunk off into the kitchen, clutching his green rucksack.

Karsten blew his nose, but it could just as easily have been a trumpet. "The lad looks like he could kill someone. What's up, Stig?"

Stig brushed off some specks of snow from his hair and jumper. "It's all sorted. Gustav just needed a bit of direction. Teenage stuff."

"He's not got himself involved in any bad business, has he? Because I told him last time that—"

"No, nothing criminal."

Karsten sneezed again. "Nothing criminal yet, you mean—"

Stig watched Gustav as he headed through the kitchen door. "He's okay, Karsten, really. Just give him a chance to find his feet." Stig reached behind the bar and hung a bunch of keys on his personal hook. "Can't stand here chatting. I'd better go and give Lisbeth some help in the kitchen. That *stegt flæsk* smells fantastic!"

"A beer for you, Stig?"

"No, you know me, Karsten. Never drink on the job. Maybe later, when I've finished." He disappeared into the kitchen.

"Now – talking of favourite foods… Do you want to hear a joke?" Karsten asked, taking a quick glance over his shoulder at Lisbeth, his wife, who was just disappearing into the hotel kitchen with a teetering pile of dirty plates.

"Oh, go on then," groaned Lea. Karsten had an endless supply of jokes. Most of which he recycled, added to and retold at length. Ninety-nine times out of a hundred they were Aarhus jokes – where the people of Aarhus, Denmark's second largest city, are portrayed as being downright daft.

"Well, a Mexican, an Italian and a man from Aarhus" – here we go, thought Lea – "are working on the top floor of a skyscraper. At 12 noon they go outside, sit on the edge and open their lunchboxes. The Mexican says, 'Please let it not be chili con carne again. If it's chili con carne I'm going to jump!' The Italian says, 'Please let it not be spaghetti. If it's spaghetti again, I'm going to jump!' The guy from Aarhus says, 'Please let it not be liver pâté. If it's *leverpostej* again, I'm going to jump!' So the Mexican takes one look at his lunch and says, 'Ai, ai ai! Chili con carne!' and jumps off. The Italian takes one look at his lunch and says, 'Mamma Mia! Spaghetti!' and jumps. The guy from Aarhus takes one look at his lunch and says '*Åh nej! Leverpostej!*' and jumps. And lands – splat - on top of the other two. It's all one big mess of hands, legs and feet," beamed Karsten, stopping the dialogue for a millisecond to take a quick breath.

Bent took a quick sup of his half pint. Lea pounced. She had spotted Lisbeth behind Karsten's shoulder, this time emerging from the kitchen with a bowl of steaming potatoes and a giant sauceboat of parsley sauce. "Lisbeth, can we put in an order for two *stegt flæsk*, please? I'll be dead from hunger before he gets to the end of this one!"

Karsten continued on, unabashed, "So it's all a big mess of bodies and they have a joint funeral. The widows are standing

41

around the graves and the Mexican's wife says, 'I don't understand! Why didn't Diego tell me he didn't like chili con carne?' The Italian's wife says, 'I don't understand! Why didn't Mario tell me he didn't like spaghetti? It's was his Mama's recipe!' The wife from Aarhus says, 'I don't understand! Jens always made his own packed lunch!'"

Bent screeched with laughter, "Karsten, every time you tell that one, it gets better and better!"

Lisbeth, who was setting a neighbouring table, looked up and shook a fork at them, "Hey! Don't forget I'm from Aarhus!"

"Not to worry, Lisbeth, my love," Karsten winked, "I'll explain the joke to you later!"

# CHAPTER 10

Kenneth and Henrik appeared at the bar and were waved over by Bent and Lea, who had been keeping a couple of seats for them. Lea received a large hug plus a peck on the cheek. Bent received the same, along with the Frandsens' usual greeting – which Lea had heard almost as often as Karsten's jokes – "Hello there, Bent – didn't recognise you with your clothes on!" They squeezed into their seats and Henrik looked adoringly at the plates piled high with *stegt flæsk*. Thick fried belly pork was a rare treat for them (the only bacon allowed in the Frandsen fridge being authentic Italian *pancetta*).

"Well, *skål*." Kenneth raised his glass of Amarone, waited for the others in turn to do the same, made eye contact with each one, and then sipped. "So, Bent, when are you finally going to get the door of the storage hut fixed? I had to rescue Ellen yesterday. Another half hour in there and the poor dear would probably have started on that dusty old bottle of *Gammel Dansk!*"

Bent put down his half pint, "Ah, well, that's a tricky one. I started on it last week, but the whole door needs to come off and my sciatica is giving me gip right now. I saw Stig out in the car park just before and that got me thinking that I should probably ask him to give me a hand – after all, he knows that storage hut like the back of his hand."

"Remember that we're here, too, if you need a hand, Bent." Lea was rapidly feeling the first, very soothing effects of her white wine after the long, cold cycle ride and was therefore in a particularly generous mood this evening.

"Thanks, Lea Mus, and cheers to that! But what I really need is a big, strong man."

"Well," quipped Henrik, looking directly at Lea, "we could all use one of those, couldn't we, dear!"

"You can say that again!" She poured some more parsley sauce over her potatoes.

"Leave some for the rest of us, Lea dear!"

Lea winked back at Henrik. "Leave some what, Henrik? Parsley sauce? Or big strong men?"

"Ha ha – touché, my dear!"

Bent tried to call a bit of order to the proceedings. "I'm sure Stig will help me. So if any of you see him again before I do, tell him I want a word, okay?"

Kenneth quickly refilled his glass with Amarone. "Stig? Why should we see him before you do?"

"I'm just saying, if you do happen—"

"I really don't think that's at all likely. I mean we're sitting here enjoying our meal. And he's working out back and—"

Bent sighed. "Okay, okay, just forget it!"

Henrik put a reassuring arm around Kenneth. "Relax, *skal*! You really are on edge tonight."

"Speaking of big, strong men," Henrik was now out of his seat and waving, "look at who just walked into the bar!"

Lea, smiling, turned around and saw a very familiar figure smiling over at them. What on earth was he doing there? The smile disappeared from her face and she felt a sudden heat working its way up from her chin to her temples. Only in part due to the extra bowl of steaming potatoes Lisbeth had just placed on their table. "Bent, is that M—" Please, Lord, don't let him come over.

"Yes, Lea Mus, it's Mads. Didn't I tell you?"

No, Bent, you bleeding well didn't… Lea passed the sauce boat to Henrik and tried to avoid Bent's eyes.

"He's renting a place down on Strandvejen while he looks for a flat in Strandvig."

Henrik sat down with a crash. "Oh, how wonderful! And he looks fantastic in that leather jacket, very James Dean. Get him over and let's drink to his return!"

"Yes, let's drink to that!" Kenneth lifted his glass of Amarone, and was disappointed to see that it already seemed to be half-empty. He lifted up the bottle from the table and filled his own glass to the brim.

Bent stood up and tried to beckon Mads over, but diverted by the sight of his old friend Stig, turned away and sat down at the bar. Saved! Breathe, Lea. Slowly, breathe slowly!

"But Bent, I thought he was living with that woman, Pernille, in Copenhagen?" said Henrik, rather piqued he wasn't au fait with the latest news.

Bent nodded. "It didn't work out for him, did it. But we all saw that coming didn't we? Seems that when our Mads was out playing football, Pernille was out playing the field."

The bitch! The heat in Lea's face was now matched by a slow heat rising in her chest.

"Bitch!" said Henrik, "I knew that Pernille was trouble. Well good riddance to her. There's nothing worse than dishonesty in a relationship!"

The others nodded their agreement. Kenneth shifted nervously in his seat. And asked Lisbeth, in a very small voice, to bring them another bottle of Amarone.

# CHAPTER 11

Lea was halfway out the door of the ladies toilets, when she suddenly changed her mind and went back in, leaving the door slightly ajar. Why was it so hot in here tonight? And why on earth didn't Bent tell her about Mads? She would bloody kill him. Lea wasn't usually the type to worry about her appearance and most mornings she'd leave the house without any makeup on and apply some eyeliner, mascara and lip-gloss when she got to the council offices. But, given that Mads had made a dramatic reappearance, it wouldn't hurt to reapply her lipstick, would it? She looked at herself in the mirror and fanned her face. It was a relief to get away from the music and raised voices.

Maybe she should comb her hair a little? And a little spritz of perfume wouldn't go amiss. Lea removed her gloves and scarf from her handbag and placed them on the counter beside the sink. She had just located her lipstick and eyeliner which, of course, were hiding at the very bottom of the bag under the remains of yesterday's lunch when she heard whispering outside in the corridor. She slowly peeked out. It was Kenneth. Why on earth was he whispering? He was leaning in towards someone. And who was he talking to?

There was a creaking sound behind her, coming from the side door to the car park, so she pulled her head quickly back behind the toilet door. But no footsteps came. The whispering continued. So Lea decided to peek out again.

Kenneth had now moved slightly. He had moved away from the centre and the glare of the corridor lights, and was standing in the shadows, almost pressed against the wall. Lea could see the person standing opposite him. It was Stig. Kenneth had his wallet open and he was handing over a bundle of notes.

"Here, this should be enough".

What the ….?

Stig counted the notes. "So you're absolutely sure he hasn't twigged yet, Kenneth?"

"No, and let's try and keep it that way! You know what Henrik is like. He'll kill me if he finds out. First he'll kill me and then he'll come and kill you!"

Stig laughed and put the money in the back pocket of his jeans. "Don't worry, Kenneth. Your secret's safe with me! Only one more week until the Moonlight Bathe and then you're home free!"

Lea heard the words Moonlight Bathe and immediately thought of cupcakes. She would not bake bloody cupcakes!

Kenneth didn't look convinced. "Maybe this is a bad idea. We could cancel—"

"It's too late to cancel now, Kenneth! Look, just leave it all to me. That's what we arranged."

"But I can just picture his face when he realises what's going on—"

Stig smiled. "When the time comes, he won't know what's hit him. Relax, Kenneth – go get yourself a glass of wine and leave it all to me!" Stig clapped Kenneth on the shoulder and went back into the bar.

Kenneth took a deep breath, checked his watch and disappeared into the gents toilets.

Lea stood in the doorway of the toilets, trying to make sense of what she had just seen. What on earth was—

"Hi, Lea!" Lea felt a heavy hand on her shoulder and jumped. She turned round to find Mads standing right behind her. Mads stood there, waiting for a reply, but none came. He moved a little closer. "It's good to see you. Sorry – did I give you a fright?"

"Um, no, not at all," she lied furiously. Don't panic, don't panic, Lea. "I was just… I was… Bent told me that you're thinking of moving back to Strandvig?"

"Yes, Pernille and I broke up at the end of summer. Didn't you hear?"

Lea managed to shake her head.

"I thought I would keep the flat and stay on in Copenhagen, but it just doesn't feel right. I never really fit in there. To be honest, I really miss Strandvig." He fixed his large brown eyes on Lea. "There are a lot of things I miss about this place."

Why did he have to look at her like that? She couldn't breathe. "Yes. Oh well, it was good to bump into you. See you down at the Vikings, I expect?"

"Actually, Lea, I was wondering if you wanted to come over for a drink. I'm staying at the old Kayak Club."

"I don't know. I'm really busy at work this week—"

"How about right now?" he insisted, "I've even got a bottle of white chilling in our old fridge. Can you believe it's still working after all these years? I can be there in, say, 20 minutes?"

"Now? Right now? That's really kind of you, Mads. But I've got a really early start tomorrow".

"Well, if you change your mind," he said, placing an arm on her shoulder, "you know where to find me. Day or night, Lea."

Lea felt a zing from her arm down to her toes. "Thanks, Mads but I'd really better get back to the others. They're waiting for me. Goodnight!" She tried to pull back from him, but he kept his arm on her shoulder.

"Goodnight, Lea". He kissed her gently – just a second too long – on the cheek and headed out the side door to the car park. Lea, alone in the corridor, caught a sudden draught of freezing air. It felt good.

# CHAPTER 12

"Well, I don't know about you lot, but I'm absolutely stuffed," said Henrik, patting his round belly with his chubby fingers. "If I eat one more piece of belly pork, I will literally burst!" But he ignored his own warning, threw caution to the wind and managed to rescue the very last strip of pork as Ida cleared away the large oval platter. And popped it into his mouth, licking his lips and enjoying every last grain of salt.

"Who's for dessert, then?" asked Ida. "We've got *citronfromage*. And the *æbletrifli* is really good tonight." She looked around the table and found the weak link in the chain. "Henrik?"

"*Citronfromage* and *æbletrifli* – both of them? Wow, that lovely new chef of yours is certainly pulling out all the stops tonight!" Henrik was torn. He had overdosed on the belly pork, but perhaps lemon mousse, smooth and slightly tart would be a good antidote? Then again, lightly cooked apples layered with crunchy pieces of crushed macaroon, and topped with freshly whipped cream was one of his favourite – if not very favourite – desserts. And the new chef didn't look like the type to be mean with the cream. Being a man of a similar, rather portly stature.

Ida could see him hesitating and went in for the kill. "If it's any help, Henrik, the trifle is served in a little jar. And topped with grated bitter chocolate…"

"Oooooo, yes! Thank you, Ida!" Henrik was sold. He was a sucker for anything served in a jar. This new chef certainly knew his stuff and the way to his customers' hearts.

Ida laughed, "You won't be disappointed. Anyone else?"

49

Bent looked at Kenneth's plate, "What's up with you tonight? You've been restless since you got here. Off your food?"

"I am feeling a bit off colour, Bent. Maybe the flu coming on?" said Kenneth, hurriedly. "But I'll take another glass of Amarone, please Ida. I don't really want one, you know, but it'll probably help to nip this thing in the bud. Starve a fever, feed a cold, and all that."

Bent raised his eyebrows.

Ida looked down at the table, committing the order to her memory. "So that's one *æbletrifli*, a glass of Kenneth's usual and coffees for Lea and Bent then," she said, about to leave the table.

"Oh, and maybe," said Henrik, touching her arm gently and whispering in her ear, "just a couple of chef's delicious *petits fours* to nibble on."

# CHAPTER 13

Ida carefully removed the candle holders and vases from the tables and lined them up on the serving trolley closest to the bar. "That's great, Ida love!" shouted Karsten. "Just you get going now – it's getting really late and you have gymnasium tomorrow, don't you?"

Ida smiled and nodded. "Yes, but I'll be here again on Monday. Just ring if you need me before then. I could do with the extra money!"

"Couldn't we all, love", shouted Johnny, who was standing behind the till and totalling up the days' takings. Ten minutes earlier he'd changed the music to John Mogensen's *'Allerbedste'* — the signal to the local punters that it was time to pay up and drink up.

"Okay, then." Ida picked up her coat and was about to put it on when a loud vibrating noise came from her pocket. *Zzzzzzz. Zzzzzzz. Zzzzzzzz.*

Johnny was getting ready to shout something inappropriate, when Karsten put his hand firmly over his mouth. "Leave her alone, Johnny, she's a nice kid. Just let her get home."

Ida, unaware of what was going on behind her, hurriedly pulled out her telephone and looked at the screen. She seemed confused and looked at it again, more closely this time and paused for a second. She started to key in a few strokes, changed her mind and switched it off, quickly putting it back in her coat pocket. Martin had to be crazy. It was really late and she really didn't want to get—

Ida's telephone buzzed again. This time she stole a glance behind her, read the message and texted a reply, before zipping up her coat. She grabbed her bike helmet and was half way towards the side door when Lisbeth stopped her.

"Wait up, poppet! Is everything okay?"

Ida reddened. "Yes, I'm fine, Lisbeth. Just on my way home now." She looked slightly hesitant. "Unless, that is, you wanted me to do something else..?"

"Oh, no, poppet. You've done a great job! I just wondered, are you biking home alone?" Lisbeth was immediately in Mother Hen mode.

Ida looked embarrassed. "Yes. But it's okay, I'll be fine on my own. Really. I'm only ten minutes along the coast road." She pointed at her helmet and smiled. "And I've got my helmet. Safety first!"

"Where is he?"

"Where's who?"

"Gustav?"

Ida was caught unawares, "Gustav? I don't know." She turned her head towards the kitchen door. "He wasn't in the kitchen. Out the back maybe?"

"I really don't like the thought of you cycling on your own."

"Honestly, Lisbeth, I'll be fine. Goodnight!" Ida waved and headed out the side door, not looking back.

Lisbeth was immediately on high alert. "Karsten, have you seen Gustav?"

"Not recently, my love. I thought he was in the kitchen with you?"

"That was ages ago. He was in a right mood – wouldn't speak to anyone. On the bright side, he washed the dishes faster than ever before. Did you speak to him?"

"No, my love. Stig said it was best to leave him alone. They had had a bit of a bust up out in the car park when Gustav turned up for work tonight. But Stig said it was best we gave him some time to cool off—"

"I thought you said the other day you were going to give him a warning. That's the third time in a row that he's been late. And now he's gone off without a word to anyone? Maybe I should call his mum—"

"Now don't worry that pretty little Aarhus head of yours—"

Lisbeth looked like she was going to throw the heap of dirty tablecloths she was holding onto Karsten's head. "I'll give you Aarhus!"

Lea whispered to Bent, "And on that note, it's high time we did a disappearing act!"

Lisbeth clutched the tablecloths to her bosom and turned to Lea. "I hope she'll be alright."

Lea patted Lisbeth's arm. "Ida? Don't worry, Lisbeth. She's a big girl, she'll be fine. Besides, Bent and I are heading that way too. We'll keep an eye out for her."

Lisbeth put the damask tablecloths down on a table and started folding them. Even if they were dirty, she still liked them to be neatly stacked before they went off to the laundry service. "A good worker. And just a lovely, lovely girl. Pretty too! No wonder Gustav is all silly when he's around her."

"Gustav's got a crush on her? Is that what you think's going on?"

"Well, he has been acting all strange recently. I think Gustav's all smitten with our Ida. Typical teenage boy. Gone straight to his head!"

Bent nodded. "He wouldn't be the first and he certainly won't be the last. Ha ha, it's a beautiful thing, young love. Though I'm not so sure that Ida is aware of his, um, affections."

Lea smiled. "She's probably blissfully unaware. Gustav's got a funny way of showing it, all moody and shy. Anyway, Ida doesn't look like she has time for a boyfriend. Studying full-time and working here and for that Brix family. I don't know how she stands it." Lea rolled her eyes. Maria Brix was all too known to Lea and her colleagues at Strandvig Council. Maria had pestered the Day Care

53

department for days on end when, at six months, the twins were finally old enough to attend crèche. Her husband, Martin, worked at some fancy PR bureau in Copenhagen, but no-one could figure out what Martin actually did there. Though it seemed to require some rather showy gentlemen's apparel (indeed, rather racy by Strandvig village standards), long days at his desk and even longer nights frequenting the various hot spots of Copenhagen. Invariably in the company of young, attractive females. Strandvig had dubbed the pair 'High Maintenance Maria' and 'Martin the Peacock', and some villagers proclaimed that they had already spotted the first ugly cracks in the façade of the otherwise 'perfect' family.

Bent smiled. "Patience of a saint, she has, young Ida. Elvira calls her the Mother Teresa of Strandvig. Did you know Elvira is her grandmother?"

"Really, Bent?" Lea had never made the connection before.

"Elvira, yes. A fine looking woman herself! Very sound of mind and body—"

"Oh, Bent, you and your harem. You're the giddy limit!"

Bent pretended to look offended. "You know what they say. I may be mean, but I'm very generous with my body!"

"Oh, away with you, you old fool!" Lisbeth gave him a playful swipe on the shoulder. "Get home to bed!"

Bent looked at his watch. "You know what else they say, Lisbeth. If you're not in bed by midnight…go home!" He chortled and gave the thumbs up to Karsten, who returned the gesture.

Lea looked at her watch and started pulling on her coat, but didn't bother to button it up. She was still flushed from earlier and was looking forward to getting outside into the cool air. If she didn't know better, she'd blame the early menopause. Damn that Mads Sørensen! She picked up her bag from the floor, dumped it on the table and rummaged around for her bike keys. Out came her two-metre long grey lambswool scarf, her thermal gloves and hat, makeup bag, diary, two water bottles – both of them almost empty, her half-munched salmon sandwich from the day before, a couple of untouched fig bars and various hairbrushes as well as two small white envelopes. Damn! She had promised her colleague to drop the letters off personally on the way to the Kro tonight… Oh well, she would do it on the way home. She could do with the exercise and it would be a good way to cool off. Now, where were those keys when she needed them?

Meanwhile Bent was pulling out his yellow beanie from his pocket and zipping his overcoat all the way up. With his red nose, he looked rather like a little gnome. All he needs now is a fishing rod, thought Lea. She had better not tell him that. Then again, he and his overinflated ego could probably take it.

Lisbeth gave them both a squeeze and a hug and went back to folding tablecloths while Karsten sent them on their way with his parting shot. "Leaving already, folks? Here's one for the road—"

Lea groaned. "Goodnight Karsten!"

Karsten looked hurt. "Don't you want to hear it?"

Bent adjusted his beanie and looked over at Lea. "You can't leave the man hanging like that, Lea Mus…"

"Oh, all right. But get on with it, will you? We haven't got all night."

"Ha ha – that's what she said last night!" shouted Johnny, still standing at the till.

Karsten grinned. "Okay, why do the people of Aarhus walk in the middle of the road?"

John Mogensen's throaty voice echoed around the room. *"Life is short, life is short, think very carefully before you throw it away…"*

Lea shook her head and waved the envelopes at Bent. "I'm not hanging around for this, Bent, I need to get these posted. See you all later!"

Karsten tried to stop her leaving. "Hold on, Lea, my love. You haven't heard the punchline yet!"

Lea sighed. "Karsten, I know the punchline. We all know the punchline. We've heard it a thousand—"

"They walk in the middle of the road because they're scared of the wild flowers in the verge! Ha ha!"

Lea covered her eyes with one hand. "Ugh. Let's go, Bent. Quick! Before he has the chance to think of another. Goodnight all!"

## CHAPTER 14

The Strandhøj car park was now deserted apart from the hotel minivan and the ten black Raleigh guest bikes that stood neatly side-by-side under the hotel carport. Sparkling with hard frost. Lea gave Bent a quick squeeze and then fumbled with her bike lock. "I need to drop off these two letters on my way home – they're both on that street beside the riding club, so I'll see you down at the Vikings tomorrow, okay?"

"Sure you don't want me to cycle with you, Lea Mus?"

Lea looked up and stared at him. "Cycle with me?"

"Well, it's very dark."

"Bent, it's dark here by three o'clock in the afternoon. I have regulation bike lights and I know how to use them!"

"And it's very late, Lea Mus."

"Yes, I know. But it won't take me long. Besides, it's in the opposite direction to you."

"I know, Lea Mus. But I don't mind."

"Bent, I'll be fine, I promise. I'm a big girl, too, remember?"

"I know, I know. But it would be nice if you had a good, strong man to look after you, Lea Mus."

Lea didn't move for a second, then straightened up. "Bent, would you mind not calling me 'Lea Mus'?"

"But I thought you liked it?"

Lea looked down, started to fumble with her keys and sighed loudly, "Well, I just don't like it so much anymore." She looked up at him. "Honestly, Bent. I'm not thirteen – I passed the thirty mark long ago! Do you mind?" Yes, this year things were going to be different. She was a big girl. She would not allow herself to be

57

walked over. Or bake cupcakes! Or let other people make decisions for her. It had to stop!

Bent looked down at his shoes. "Okay, sweetheart, I'll try and remember."

He shuffled his feet and made black marks on the shiny white tarmac. He decided to try again. "It was good to see Mads again."

Lea was now fully engaged in brushing off some thick frost from her bike saddle and refused to look up.

"He seems to be on top form. He always was a good looking lad and now he's a handsome man."

Continued silence from Lea. Bent decided not to push it any further. "Oh, well, safe home, then, sweetheart. Sweet dreams!"

He watched Lea sprint away down the coastal road. She didn't look back. What on earth had got into the lassie? Bent looked around the deserted car park, sighed deeply and pulled a package out of his pocket.

## CHAPTER 15

Lea kept her head down on the coastal road. It really was the coldest night of the New Year. Anyway, dropping the letters off should only take a few extra minutes each way and she could already see a faint glow up ahead. She thought of Ida – young, sweet Ida – and hoped that she had managed to get home safely. She imagined Ida in her pyjamas and fluffy socks, all tucked up at home in bed, surrounded by a collection of well-hugged, snuggly rabbits. No scratch that. Ida was also a big girl. In reality Ida was more likely to be sitting in her darkened bedroom with her iPhone, texting. Texting with...Gustav? It hadn't really crossed her mind before, but now she thought about it, Lisbeth might be on to something. Was he smitten with Ida? True enough, Gustav had been acting strangely the past few weeks. But he wasn't normally so sullen, so downright rude. Tonight had been really out of character. A love-struck teenager, maybe that's what's up with him?

Come to think of it, what was up with everyone tonight? If she didn't know better, she would have put it down to a full moon. But the Moonlight Bathe was next week... Ugh, cupcakes! Damn that Holy Helle! Why didn't she speak up for herself this morning? When had she ever, ever mentioned a passion for baking cupcakes? She was so tired of being a doormat.

The Moonlight Bathe! The close encounter with Mads had pushed Kenneth and Stig's conversation right to the very back of her mind. What was all that about? Kenneth had literally been on the edge of his seat. Should she mention it? *Oh, hi Kenneth! Was just wondering if you'd like to share with me why you were handing over wads of money to Stig...* No. And she wouldn't mention it to Bent. He was in

59

her bad books right now. She was a big girl, wasn't she? There was a rumbling noise behind her and a lorry thundered past, bringing with it a blast of icy air. Brrrrrrr! Suddenly she wasn't so sure. Oh, to be tucked up at home, surrounded by cuddly bunnies!

Lea regretted not putting on her hat and gloves back at the hotel car park, but at that point she had still been flushed (and sizzling) from her close encounter with Mads. And she had been desperate for a quick getaway from Bent. He was another one. What on earth had gotten into him tonight? Why didn't he tell her that Mads was back in town? Bent of all people should have warned her. He was supposed to be her friend. And now Bent was suddenly all interested in her love life. Or lack thereof... Aaaaargh! Bloody men.

The owner of the riding club lived above the stables and the yellow lights coming from the riding club paddock were a welcoming sight. She'd turn off the road in a minute's time. Lea kept pedalling, reached into her handbag, which was squashed into the front basket, and pulled out a glove. The first glove went on okay, with a bit of help from her teeth. The second one...didn't. Lea had a surreal out-of-body experience and saw the whole thing in slow motion. She lost her balance, one foot slipped and the other jammed on the pedal, braking hard. Too hard. The bike swerved, began to topple and two excruciatingly slow seconds later Lea was lying on the cycle path with the bike on top of her.

Bugger! Don't cry, Lea! She lay on the path, breathing heavily. Don't cry! She rolled over and lay flat, listening. Not a sound from the road, no cars or passers-by. No, she wouldn't cry, she was past crying. She was fuming! She stood up slowly, swearing like a sailor under her breath and looked up and down the coastal road. Still no-one around and no activity from the riding club. Thank goodness for that, the last thing she needed right now was a witness to her own stupidity. Lea picked up her bike and inspected it. She couldn't see any obvious damage, but then again, the only light provided on the bike path came from the moon.

There was a blinking light beside her. Damn. Her telephone must have jettisoned from her handbag at the same time as she had jettisoned from her bike. Oh well, at least it was lying face upwards. She picked it up and checked it for damage. She could hear it ringing. Ugh, she had pressed the call button by mistake and it was calling the last person on the list. Bent. The very last person she wanted to see right now. She'd never hear the end of it. *"I told you I would cycle with you, Lea Mus. It was very dark and cold. You really do need a big, strong man to look after you, Lea Mus."* Bla, bla, bla. Before she could stop the call, it went to his answerphone.

"Well hullo there, ladies! You've come to the right place! Bent Bang at your service. I'm busy right now, but leave a messa—" Hmph! So much for him being there if she needed help. Not that she wanted his help right now, just the opposite. *"I'm busy right now..."*

God knows what he was up to. He was probably 'busy' with one of his many lady friends. How the heck did he do it? And at his age? She switched off her phone and threw it back into her handbag. One of the water bottles had rolled on to the pavement and the sad remains of the half-eaten salmon sandwich were spread beside it. Lea retrieved the water bottle, but decided to leave the bread and cucumber for the birds' breakfast.

Lea wanted to sob but took a couple of deep breaths. Oh to be in a warm, cosy bed, surrounded by fluffy rabbits! She decided to pull herself together and took a swig of the water left in the bottle. But her hands were shaking and most of it missed her mouth and dribbled down her neck. She bent over, choking and noticed that her whole right side, including her coat and black jeans were now white with frost. Bloody hell, what a right state she was in. She dusted herself off using the offending glove and cursed again.

*"Life is short, life is short, think very carefully before you throw it away..."*

To hell with water, she could really use a medicinal whisky. (Even though she didn't drink whisky.) The image of Mads, waiting

61

for her, swinging a chilled bottle of white, suddenly popped into her mind. Now she was livid. That conceited over-confident swine. Why on earth shouldn't she have that drink with him? And that was her fridge! She could feel the heat rising inside of her again. She was a grown woman who could look after herself. *"You know where to find me. Day or night, Lea."* She would give him *"day or night, Lea"*. She would knock on his damn door right now. She would have that drink and then leave. Cool as a cucumber. That would show him.

She picked up her bike, threw the water bottle into her basket and wrapped her scarf around her neck three times. She limped across the coastal road, pushing her bike in front of her, cursing under her breath. And headed back towards the Kayak Club.

## CHAPTER 16

The journey down to the Kayak Club had only taken a couple of minutes but felt like an eternity. Lea's rage quickly turned to a slow simmer. And she wasn't quite so confident by the time she reached the driveway of the Kayak Club. But by now her right elbow was beginning to ache from the fall and her whole body was freezing. She desperately wanted to warm up – and couldn't care less where that might be. Preferably with a large mug of hot tea rather than a chilled glass of Mad's cheap supermarket plonk.

Two or three cars had passed by, but otherwise there was no sound, apart from the hum of the flickering lamppost and the crunch of her long winter boots on the gravel. Lea leant her bike up against the Kayak Club wall and didn't bother to lock it. She fought for a second with her handbag and wrenched it out of the front basket. Breathe, Lea. She shook her hair back and rang the doorbell. Riiiiiiiiiing. No reply. Riiiiiiiiiing. Still no reply. What the..? She took a step back from the door and glanced left and right, up and down. All the lights were off. Riiiiiiiiiiing. Riiiiiiiiiiing. Riiiiiiiiiiing. She felt the rage returning and pulled on the front door handle, rattling it for all she was worth and knocking with her fists on the door. But the door was solid and there was no noise from within. I don't bloody believe this!

Lea turned around to leave and realised for the first time that the driveway was empty. That should have been a giveaway. No sign of Mad's blue Volvo. Or any other car for that matter. Well, of all the bloody cheek... This was the very last time, Mads Sørensen!

Lea could feel tears starting to prick at the back of her eyes. Her arm was hurt, yes, but so was her pride: a mixture of cold anger and blazing hot embarrassment. She threw her handbag back into the bike basket, grabbed the bike and sped off. As she turned out of the Kayak Club driveway she glanced back and prayed that no-one – least of all Mads – had seen her.

## CHAPTER 17

He sat in the pitch black, thinking. God, it was quiet tonight. Too quiet. He would have welcomed some noise to give him some company and drown out his own thoughts. What had just happened? He leaned forward and put his head in his hands, rocking himself forwards and backwards. It had all gone wrong. Terribly wrong. He hadn't meant to do it. Well, not that last part. That hadn't been the plan at all. His head pounded. It had just sort of...happened. He closed his eyes and wished his head would stop pounding. He continued to rock back and forth, the repetitive movement strangely soothing.

Had anyone seen him? Think, now. This was important. He raised his head and stared out into the darkness. The pounding began to subside. He took a deep breath, then a swig. Had anyone actually seen him? Seen them? No, there were only a few cars on the road tonight. When you thought about it, there had been nothing to see. Nothing out of the ordinary. For God's sake, this was Strandvig after all. Nothing ever happened in Strandvig.

He began to feel better. He put his head in his hands again, the rocking motion was meditative. Think, now. Had anyone heard? If you thought about it, there had been very little sound. Not at all like on the telly or in films. It had all been over so quickly. Strange that it had been so very easy. It was an accident after all. That's it. It was a tragic accident. That's all. Nothing ever happened in Strandvig so, of course, it was an accident. No-one would think otherwise.

Anyhow there was no way back for him now. He shivered and took another sip. What's next? Next? There was nothing for him to do but keep calm and ride it out. He stood up and inspected his jacket. No visible signs at all. He stretched and yawned. And put the whole episode to the back of his mind. Just a tragic accident that would be reported in *Kystbladet*, right along with this week's supermarket offers. Case closed.

# CHAPTER 18

Karin was kneading. On Fridays she always made a double batch of dough, though she wouldn't be eating any of the bread herself. Not that she didn't love it. Quite the opposite in fact, it seemed to love her back. It especially loved her hips and her waist and her calves and...well, all of her really. So it was either the bread or the gym. And, as Karin was quite the couch potato, she simply made do with the heavenly smell of the bread when it came out of the oven, topped off with the looks on the children's faces when they tucked into it. Gone were the days when homemade bread or rolls were an everyday occurrence in the lives of Danish children. These days both mum and dad worked full time. And stressed out full time, whether they were delivering the kids at 7.30 am in the morning or picking them up at 5 pm. Karin thought of little Filippa. She was invariably the last child to be collected – the poor little mite – when Karin was going through her daily closedown routine of switching off all the lights and locking up.

The smell of warm, baking bread spread a guaranteed blanket of *hygge* over the nursery. Especially on these winter days, when the contrast between the cold and dark outside and the cosy, candlelit glow inside was even sharper. She knew the kids would tear into the rolls and liver pâté this afternoon. With gusto, just as they did with everything they encountered, be it food, toys or insects in the playground. Ah, to be a child again! But there would be no more white bread for Karin. Only good old Danish ryebread. Rich in taste, and very definitely high in fibre. And, when you thought about it (which she tried not to too much), not such a very bad substitute after all.

After the first rise, Karin would split the dough into two. Shape one half into rolls for the kids' afternoon snack (and remembering to keep one back for an extra treat for little Filippa at 4.45 pm) and freeze the other half. Come Monday morning, when it was Jannick's day to open the nursery, all he had to do was remove the bag from the freezer and let it defrost on the counter. Then later he'd let the kids help him, pulling off chunks of dough and roughly shaping them into rolls with their tiny fingers. A great teachable moment and exercise for their fine motor skills.

Karin was growing very fond of young Jannick. She'd misjudged him when he first arrived at *Æblegården*. He looked like a big kid with his mop of curls – well, he was a big kid. Only twenty-two, still very naïve and yet to learn the ways of the world. But he'd proved to be such a valuable assistant. Karin didn't readily hand over the keys (much less the running) of the nursery, but Jannick was intelligent, calm and compassionate. A hit with both the kids and their parents. Who were beginning to queue up with their requests for private babysitting, with Mathilde and Mathias' parents very firmly in pole position. Yes, Jannick would be sorely missed at the end of his placement.

Karin took her mug of Nescafé and headed into the warm laundry room. Thank goodness Stig had fixed the radiator – he could always be relied upon. She wondered what he was up to this morning – clearing the paths at Strandhøj, no doubt. She shivered – well, hopefully he was well bundled up. She filled up the basket of nappies on the shelf above the changing table and made a mental note to order more disposable wipes. She removed a load of bibs from the dryer and looked out the window to the playground. Snow was coming down heavily outside and she enjoyed folding the red towelling bibs, still warm from the dryer. She finished her coffee and checked her watch. Best get a move on, not long till kick-off.

Karin took her mug and three single socks and one welly boot – why was there always a lone welly boot in the electric drying cabinet? – then headed back to the cloakroom. The large wicker basket was already overflowing with scarves, lone slippers, cardigans and bicycle helmets. As well as various dummies, the Play Mobil pirate ship, pieces of paper with crayon doodles on them, a large T-Rex and various Lego bricks. She removed the pirate ship and Lego and took them into Red Room.

The heat from Red Room was stifling so she opened the windows for some fresh, icy air and decided to finish her coffee out on the playground. She quickly swapped her slip-on sneakers for her crocs, pulled on her purple, full-length, goose-down winter coat and headed out to make a quick inspection. In the summer months it was part of her routine to make an inspection every single morning. The long, light nights of Danish summer always had the same effect on the local teens. It somehow gave them the urge to jump over the nursery fence in the evenings and use the playground as a base for a party. So you never knew exactly what you were going to discover in the playhouses the next morning. Usually it was empty beer bottles or Bacardi Breezers. Karin would carry a bag around the playground with her, collecting the empties. And on *tur dag* on Thursday, when the kids were out for their walk, they'd take the bag with them and get the deposit money on the bottles. It didn't amount to more than a few *kroner*, but the kids loved feeding the bottles, one by one, into the big, flashing, noisy recycling machine.

No sign of beer bottles this morning. Only frozen puddles. All the sand toys were in their designated tub. The twenty-five green Arla milk crates (which had been 'stolen' and repurposed as giant building blocks) were stacked in towers of four. She could hear her own voice. *"No more than four, Jannick, or they'll crash down and hurt the kids' fingers when they topple!"* She checked the shed, where all the balance bikes and trikes were piled together, and the lock was intact.

All Karin's ducks were in a row. Even the wheelbarrows and wooden carts in the carport were lined up side-by-side, like soldiers. And slowly being covered with snow. It was then she spied something out of place, huddled up in the back corner of the carport. A body, dark and motionless.

CHAPTER 19

The Carlsberg lorry pulled slowly out of the Strandhøj car park. Karsten waved to the driver and hurried back into the bar, brushing off large snowflakes from his shirtsleeves and rubbing his hands together. "Brrrrrrr!"

"Shhhhhh!" Lisbeth was perched on a chair, behind the bar, phone in hand, chatting with a fresh foodstuffs supplier. The two women hadn't exactly seen eye-to-eye when they first started working together but, twenty years of weekly phone calls later, they'd both mellowed and struck up an unusual phone friendship: they lived no more than five kilometres apart, but had never met. Their call always followed the same procedure. First they'd go through the week's order. Then moved swiftly on to the week's gossip: more often than not what the Danish Royals were wearing, doing or giving birth to.

Karsten looked at Johnny, who was busy setting tables. "Who's she on the phone to?"

"Margrethe, I think".

Karsten shrugged. "Well, that's her busy for the next half hour then. I think I preferred it when they had a mutual dislike for each other – I got more work out of her back then!"

Lisbeth peeped up. "Hey, you, I heard that!" Then she turned her chair around and went back to work with Margrethe: seeing which of them could remember the most middle names of the Crown Prince's five children. Each child had three middle names. Lisbeth was currently in the lead and thoroughly enjoying her chance to shine by being able to remember the more exotic middle names given to the Royal twins. Princess Josephine had 'Ivalo' and

70

Prince Vincent was given 'Minik'. Both relatively unknown names in Denmark. At least, that is, until they were read out at the Royal christening, and sent ripples through the highly expectant community of Danish mothers-to-be. Ivalo and Minik were very common Greenlandic names. So their selection had been a very deliberate right royal salute to the Greenlanders and Greenland: Denmark's territory above the Arctic Circle. Lisbeth bobbed her head, "I know, Margrethe. Vincent Frederik Minik Alexander is a mouthful!"

Meanwhile Karsten took a double take at Johnny. "By the way, you're in early this morning, aren't you?" He walked over and made a great show of looking Johnny up and down. "Johnny, if I didn't know better, I'd swear Martians had taken you away during the night and replaced you with an upgrade. Well, well, well – look at you all clean and tidy. What's the big occasion? Hot date tonight?"

"Nah, just want to look my best, Karsten. Never know when opportunity is going to come knocking on your door, do you?"

Karsten sniffed the air. "And what's that smell?" He leant in over Johnny's shoulder and sniffed again. "*For fanden*, Johnny, you smell like a hooker's handbag!"

Johnny tried to shrug it off. "Nah, Karsten. I'm wearing clean socks today!"

Karsten laughed and slapped him on the back. Lisbeth put down the phone, "Oh, will you leave him alone, Karsten! Johnny, I think you look very nice." She smiled at him, "She must be a very lucky lady!"

Karsten started moving glasses behind the bar. "Well, it's good you're in early. The paths need salting. Can you do it when you're finished here?"

"Already done, Karsten! Saw to it when I arrived."

Lisbeth put down the phone and looked at Karsten. "Didn't Stig do it?"

"No, he didn't. Because Stig isn't here yet."

"What? Did he call?"

"Well, you've been hogging the phone for the last fifteen minutes, my love..."

"I meant before that."

"No."

"Well, have you tried calling him?" Lisbeth was beginning to worry.

"Yes, my love."

"And?"

"He didn't answer."

Lisbeth wasn't going to let it go. "Did you leave him a message?"

"Yes, my love."

She looked at her watch. "Well, that's not like Stig at all. He's so reliable."

"Lisbeth, my love... The roads are bad. Maybe he got caught somewhere. Don't worry that pretty little Aarhus head of yours!"

Lisbeth scrunched up an old cream coloured paper serviette and threw it at him. Then checked her mobile phone to see if Stig had left a message there.

"Karsten, have you tried calling *Æblegården*?"

CHAPTER 20

Mads stretched and yawned. His head was pounding and his throat was dry. He switched on the bedside lamp and cursed: it was time to make a clean start. He got up and headed towards the living room, making a path through the clothes strewn across the floor. His leather jacket was lying on the sofa, where he had thrown it last night. Mads pulled it on and walked over to the stereo. He picked up a small, white wicker basket, and started to flick through the CDs one-by-one. Then changed tactics and went straight for the one at the back. Magtens Korridorer. Of course, he should have known that she would put it right at the very back. She had always hated it.

Mads put the CD in his coat pocket, and slammed the door behind him. Next stop would be the petrol station for some coffee and bread on the way back to the Kayak Club. And perhaps even pick up a bunch of flowers for Lea.

## CHAPTER 21

*I must be mad!* Lea kept her head down and cycled against the wind as best she could. Her uniform of grey woollen hat and grey lambswool scarf were normally up to the job. But on a winter morning like this one – when just breathing in and out was painful – she had felt that it was time to bring out the big guns. It had taken her a few, frantic extra minutes to locate her old, rather sorry looking dark green, fleece earmuffs at the back of her wardrobe. Like everything else in there, the earmuffs had been pushed further and further back and had finally given up and decided to seek cover inside one of the many black tops that lurked right at the back (those same black tops that seemed to breed by the week). But after much pushing and pulling, and a few choice expletives, victory was hers. The earmuffs wrapped snuggly round the back of her head and tucked in nicely underneath her woollen hat. Cosy ears were definitely high up on the list of daily luxuries. As were her new thermal ski gloves, even if they weren't exactly the most glamorous choice for a woman of her age. And, let's be honest, Lea could no longer still describe herself as a girl. 'Young woman' was the most she could get away with these days. Yes, the gloves had been a tad expensive. But she was worth it, right? They didn't let in the cold wind like her old woollen ones had. Ugh, just listen to her. Warmth and practicality had once again trumped her sense of fashion. What was wrong with her? First the crocs and now these. She was an old maid.

Despite being swaddled like a baby in a crib, Lea's cheeks were exposed and beginning to turn a very bright shade of red. She could feel the cold wind beginning to bite the inside of her nostrils.

It tickled and made her want to sneeze. She tried to pull her scarf up over her nose. And focused her mind very firmly on the prospect of the hot sauna waiting for her. Heaven. Just the tonic she needed after being out in the cold all night. She tried not to dwell too much on the fact that the bathing steps would certainly be encrusted in a rather thick layer of ice. Even though she loved winter bathing, she would never ever get used to walking on ice with wet feet. Thankfully one of the Oldies – Bent or Ole – would already have chipped the worst ice away and sprinkled salt on the main paths.

And where was Bent? She had tried ringing him before she left the house, feeling rather guilty about being so short with him in the car park last night. But just like last night there was no reply, only his silly answering machine. That man was so hard to pin down! She could hear his voice in her head. *"Me…hard to pin down? That's what she said last night! Ha ha!"* Lea tried to ignore the image of Bent and one of his harem that popped up in her head and decided she would give him a big hug when she got to the club. Lea would be honest with him and apologise. After all, it wasn't Bent's fault that Mads had been such a jerk. As she herself had said to Bent in the car park last night, she was a big girl. And big girls should be able to manage their own problems. Especially boy problems.

The gravel spreaders had passed by only moments before. There were tiny flecks of grey on the cycle lane and, as was often the case, the cycle paths were in better shape than the roads this morning. Lea really wasn't keen on cycling on ice but, as she didn't own a car, there was no real alternative transport apart from the hourly bus that served the coastal road. The round trip would take at least an hour and a half – there was no way she could fit in a swim and still be at her council desk ready to do some work by 9 am. So bike it was.

The passing cars provided occasional flashes of warm, yellow light. She kept in the middle of the cycle path and kept her head and her speed down. Her elbow and her thigh were still smarting from the night before, so she certainly wasn't keen to take another tumble.

And she'd probably have a lovely yellow bruise to show for it. Something for the others to speculate, while they sat knee-to-knee in the sauna. Lea started to feel warmth coming back to her body. Warmth stemming from a burning feeling inside of her. *"Day or night"*, my ass. What a crook he was. And to think she had almost fallen for it. Yes, Mads Sørensen was out of her life. For ever.

# CHAPTER 22

"Morning, Karin!" Sonja was sitting in the cloakroom part of the entrance hall, quietly cheering on Asger, who was in the final stages of the painstaking process of removing his thermal ski suit and his thermal boots. Not the easiest of tasks when you're two-years old and all fingers and thumbs. Especially when you are deaf to reason and insist on wearing your gloves throughout the process. Karin put a protective hand in the space between Asger's head and the wooden cloakroom hooks when he wobbled slightly, pulling his left foot out of the trouser leg. "What's up? You look like you've just seen a ghost."

"So would you, if you'd just been in the carport." She held up a long, damp, furry brown object. "I found it lying at the back and thought it was a dead body."

"Ha ha, someone's been watching too many of those thrillers on TV! That's Oscar's ski suit, isn't it?"

Karin looked at the name label. "Bingo!"

"What was it doing in the carport?"

"Heaven only knows. His mum probably dropped it when they were on their way out last night." Droplets of water fell slowly on to the floor. "But there's no way he can wear that right now, it's completely sodding. I'll throw it in the washing machine. He can borrow one of the spare ones today."

The shuffling and panting beside them stopped. "Hey, well done, Asger! You did it all by yourself!"

Asger looked up proudly. "I've pooped!"

"Oh! That's great!" She winked at Sonja. "Onwards and upwards! Don't you just love this job?"

Sonja stood up and ironed the crease out of her back. "No better way to start the day... Come on, Asger. Let's get you changed. Give me the ski suit, Karin, I'll throw it in the wash when we're in there."

"Thanks! By the way, it's nice and cosy in the laundry room. Stig fixed the radiator yesterday." She held up her coffee mug. "Want some coffee, Sonja?"

"Music to my ears, I'd love one!"

The office phone rang and Karin turned around. "Okay, just let me answer this and I'll bring you one. If it's Maria Brix – again – demanding we only serve organic raisins, or that Mathilde and Mathias need their teeth brushed every lunchtime, I swear I will scream."

## CHAPTER 23

Lisbeth looked up from her magazine, a combination of Royal news and TV guide. She and Karsten didn't get much chance to watch TV, but they kept a copy in the reception for guests to leaf through. And for Lisbeth to coo over pictures of Royal babies, not having had any of her own. A long wail of a siren and a flash of blue had interrupted her fifth attempt to start the beginners' Sudoku on the game page. No matter how many times she tried, the figures just danced in front of her.

"Hey, lads, did you see that? An ambulance just went past!"

"Yes, my love. Well done, that was an ambulance. Two points to you!" He winked at Johnny.

Lisbeth ignored him. "But look, it's stopped. Just on the other side, in front of the Vikings!"

Karsten tried to pooh-pooh the situation. He had managed to distract Lisbeth from stressing over Stig's failure to report for duty this morning, and was keen to avoid another half hour of anxiety, speculation and extra phone calls. Especially as they would be run off their feet today and he wanted to get some work out of her. "Don't you worry, my love! Probably just Holy Helle having another one of her bloody fire drills! Yes, Sir, Sergeant Major, Sir!" he said, clicking his feet together and saluting.

Johnny craned his neck, "Probably one of the old biddies fainted when they saw Bent Bang parading his crown jewels on the bathing bridge!"

Karsten laughed, perhaps a bit too loud. "The oldest swinger in town strikes again!"

Lisbeth closed the magazine and stood up.

"Hey, Johnny, talking of ambulances," Karsten was already chuckling to himself, "how many people from Aarhus—"

Lisbeth frowned, "Karsten, really, I don't think this is the time—"

"—does it take to drive an ambulance?"

Johnny laughed. "Out with it, don't keep me in suspense!"

"Two! One to say 'Baaaaa' and one to say 'Boooo'!"

"Really, Karsten!" Lisbeth reached up and gave him a short, swift slap on the top of the head then took up position at the window.

## CHAPTER 24

The ambulance passed Lea on the way, sirens blaring. She had seen it turn on to the coastal road as she was unlocking her bike. But she hadn't realised it had been heading for the Vikings. And now, there it was again, making a U-turn and coming back down towards her. She had a bad feeling at the bottom of her stomach, which was balanced by the genuine pain she could feel in her right leg, which had started to throb. She pedalled as fast as her leg and the ice would allow. And cursed Mads, again.

The snow was fairly coming down now and, even though snowflakes were sticking to her eyelashes, she could make out a small group huddled together on the bathing jetty. The Oldies were easy to spot: slightly small in stature and slightly bent over. Bent was there too, with his bright yellow beanie hat. And she knew that last one was Holy Helle. Either that or it was a large, furry creature depositing a large brown bottle – could it be the infamous bottle of *Gammel Dansk?* – into the recycling bin.

Lea locked her bike, fished for the club key, which she kept on an old Scout lanyard in the bottom of her bathing bag and rushed towards the gate. Bent had seen her arrive and was rushing up the boards towards her, his yellow beanie-covered head bent down in an attempt to avoid the snowflakes. Lea suddenly felt a very large wave of guilt come over her. She had behaved so badly towards him at the car park last night and she could feel tears pricking at her eyes. When he opened the gate she gave him a spontaneous hug, almost knocking him over.

Bent sighed. "Oh, Lea Mus, I don't know where to start!"

"What on earth's going on? It's not Ellen, is it?"

"Ellen, Lea Mus?" Bent looked up at her, puzzled.

"The ambulance I saw just now. It was coming from here, wasn't it?"

Bent still looked confused. "Yes, but—"

"Was it for Ellen? Did she get stuck in the storage hut again?"

"What? Oh no, Lea Mus. Ellen isn't even here today." He hesitated and looked up at her, slightly lost. "Oh, I'm sorry, sweetheart, I'm not supposed to say 'Lea Mus' anymore, am I?"

Lea rubbed his arm gently and for the first time suddenly realised how old Bent actually was. He looked as though the wind had been completely knocked out of him. Someone had replaced the sprightly joker with a frail, old man.

"Oh, *pyt*, Bent, I don't care about that! Just tell me what's going on!"

"Oh, Lea Mus, I'm afraid I've got some bad news for you. Ole and Yrsa Olsen were here at 6.45 am to open up. They were on their way down the bathing steps when Yrsa spotted a body – a man – floating in the water."

"Oh my God!"

"They tried to drag him back up on to the bridge and Yrsa called an ambulance."

"How awful! Is he going to be alright?"

Bent looked away, tears in his eyes. "There was nothing they could do for him, sweetheart. Apparently he'd been in the water for hours…"

Lea felt sick. "Bent…is he dead then?"

"Yes. It's just – it's just I just can't understand it."

"Bent, who is it? Please, tell me."

Bent took Lea's gloved hands in his and looked up at her with a weary look. "I'm so sorry, Lea Mus. It was Stig."

# CHAPTER 25

Bent trudged off to the storage hut, head down against the snow, yellow beanie in hand. He couldn't fully see where he was going, because the snowflakes were coming in at full speed sideways, but he knew the layout of the bathing club so well that he could walk it in his sleep. The door would be difficult to open, of course, but he was looking forward to taking out his aggression on the defenceless piece of timber. He was angry at Stig. And what about poor Karin? Who was going to tell her?

He pulled and pushed on the handle with his small, gloved hands and kicked and cursed. He stood back to take a deep breath, blow the snowflakes off his nose and started the punishment again. He was almost disappointed when the door finally gave way, but his body was getting tired. The stale, warm scent inside caught him off guard – it was as if someone had popped open the doors of his mind – and he collapsed into a heap on one of the old wooden benches and began to sob quietly.

*Den dumme skid!* That bloody idiot! *Hva' fanden lavede han!* What the hell had he been doing?

All the memories of young Stig came flooding back. The mop-haired youngster who lived for his football. The troubled teen who had managed to get back on track. Bent watched him grow up and make his own way in life. Okay, maybe not the way his parents had expected or wanted. But Stig was a credit to the village. One of the good guys. And now this? It didn't make sense. What had Stig been doing here? Still the sobs came and Bent sat motionless, tears streaming down his face and running off his chin.

He was just taking a deep breath when he heard footsteps approaching on the boards outside. Bent sat up, quickly rubbing his eyes with his hat. A second later the door was thrown open and the light – a single bulb hanging under a 1970s rattan lampshade – was switched on. It was Holy Helle. Her silhouette was unmistakable.

"Mr Bang?!"

"Yes, Ma'am!" Bent jumped to his feet and rubbed his eyes again with his hat. Which by now was decidedly damp.

"What on earth do you think you are doing in here?"

Bent dived behind a set of dust covered shelves. "Erm, I was just fetching a bottle of *Gammel Dansk*, Ma'am! I think there's one on the back shelf here somewhere."

If Bent had been looking in the other direction, he would have seen that Helle was sporting her 'thoroughly displeased' look. But he didn't need to see her, he could hear it in the way she said "Mr Bang."

"Mr Bang. Don't you think there has been quite enough *Gammel Dansk* drunk around here for one day?"

Bent popped his little head around the shelf. "Oh, it's not for me, Ma'am."

Holy Helle didn't look convinced.

Bent coughed and carried on, regardless. "Yrsa – Mrs Olsen – has had a right shock. I thought she might be in need of a little dram to steady her nerves—"

Holy Helle preened herself slightly. "Really? Hmm, perhaps you're right. But I can inform you that she and Mr Olsen left a couple of minutes ago, so you can stop doing whatever you are doing in there and come on out. Do I make myself clear?"

## CHAPTER 26

When the swimming club reopened for business the next morning, Helle Brandt was the first Viking on the scene. According to the roster, it was officially Ole and Yrsa who should do the honours. But yesterday morning Helle had decided that she herself would take on the task of opening the secondary lock of the main gate, given the extraordinary circumstances. And they certainly were most extraordinary. There was no contingency in the Viking Club Members Rule Book for the discovery of bodies – floating, dead or otherwise – on club premises. Something, Helle pondered, that should be brought to the attention of the Viking Club Committee at their next meeting. No, scratch that – it was a matter that should be dealt with at the very earliest opportunity. Extraordinary circumstances necessitated an Extraordinary Committee Meeting. Yes, she would fire off a missive this morning. Just as soon as her current duties here at the club were fulfilled.

Yesterday's events had obviously been very distressing for them all. Helle had been slightly caught off guard by the occurrence of such an unseemly episode on her turf, but had bounced back with renewed vigour (*"stand firm in the faith, act like men, be strong"*!) and was primed, ready to take the helm, sailing steady with her iron fist. Or her calf leather-gloved fist. Ole and Yrsa, who had been smack bang in the thick of yesterday's action (and, rather sadly for Ole, very much 'hands on') were justifiably shell-shocked and clearly required a few quiet days at home, with nothing more stimulating to pass the time than a pleasant rubber or two of Bridge with their neighbours, Gorm and Karen, or an afternoon eating pancakes with their grandchildren. Though both were avid fans of Inspector Morse,

85

Midsomer Murders and Miss Marple ("Jane really would make for an excellent winter bathing companion"), watching endless repeats of those shows was certainly not going to be on the cards any time soon. The remainder of the Vikings – the Oldies, the not quite so old and the not quite so young – were in a state of shock, coupled with disbelief and grief. Many of them had known Stig since he was a nipper. Most of Strandvig drank up at the Kro, so Stig had been one of 'them'.

Helle mused on the weekend that lay ahead. Bent Bang had been most insistent – really quite verbal – that he would open today, but Helle had held fast and overruled him. She would open, today, Saturday, if Bent could take Sunday. After all, Mr Bang wasn't very likely to be rushing off to church, was he? Helle unlocked the metal gate twice, waltzed through the entrance with a swish of her fur coat and said a silent prayer for him. Dear Lord, please do what you can for Bent Bang – I know he is rather a lost cause but surely, if anyone can, you can? Help show him the way and bring him back to the flock. *"For all have sinned and fall short of the glory of God"*! Amen!

Helle headed straight for the bathing steps and tugged several times on the long length of beige polypropylene rope that was tied to the top rung. Yes, it was still secure. She lifted up the club's air thermometer, which was also attached to the bridge by a piece of string, rubbed off the frost with the tip of one of her calf leather gloves, lifted it up to her nose and peered inquisitively at the numbers. Minus 3c. She pulled up a second thermometer from the water. 0c. She lowered it slowly back into the water.

Helle's next port of call was the alcove between the ladies and gents changing huts. Next to the noticeboard was a little wooden cabinet, secured with a solid brass hook latch. This was the official residence of the Viking Club diary. Not a regular diary with days, weeks and months and the ubiquitous budget and name/address pages at the back that no-one ever used. It was an A4-size hardbacked, lined notebook. But so much more than a simple notebook: it was a testament. An intricate list of dates, times, temperatures and conditions. The men and women of the Vikings recorded their daily presence – their daily communion with the sea. An inward battle of mind over matter and a physical battle of body against time and tide. Helle fished out a pen from the back corner of the cupboard and opened the diary. Though not centuries old (Helle saw to it that a new book was ceremoniously unveiled every year on the first of January at the Vikings New Year's Dip), it had the appearance of a journal that had been through the wars. All the pages were curling up at the edges and had turned from their original white to a pale shade of brown due to their close encounter with wet fingers, strong sunshine and damp sea fog.

She took off her right glove (the wind-chill was -15°C / 5°F today, so prudence was advisable) and started writing. Today's date, her name followed by the letters FVI (First Viking In), then the water and air temperatures. But there was something odd in the line above. Yesterday's entry: Friday. There was no mention of LVO.

The LVO (Last Viking Out – responsible for checking the premises before locking up) yesterday was Mr Bang, she was sure of that. But he had omitted to write his name in the club diary. Why was that? She looked at the entry again. FVI, Yrsa and Bent Olsen. Of course – they had opened the club. And her own name, of course. The others on the bridge yesterday morning had evidently been distracted from registering their presence in the diary by the unexpected appearance and ensuing removal of dearly-departed Mr Rasmussen from club premises.

Stig Rasmussen. She pondered whether she should write in Mr Rasmussen's name, *post factum*. Or should that be *post mortem*? No, no, that wouldn't do at all. The man wasn't a Viking. He wasn't even an invited guest.

But Bent Bang was a member of the Committee. He of all people should adhere to Viking rules. He said he would close up yesterday, so why didn't he sign himself out? Moreover, what exactly had he been doing in the storage hut yesterday morning? Looking for a bottle of *Gammel Dansk*? Helle didn't buy that story of his at all.

Not for one minute. He was very clearly lying. Yes, he was up to something. Truth be told, Bent Bang was always up to something. But what was it this time? Dear Lord, was there anything that man could do right? Stand firm, Helle, stand firm.

She replaced the diary and pen, locked the cabinet and moved on to the next task, unlocking the door to the sauna. Helle stamped her feet on the mat, pulled the wooden door towards her and peaked around inside. Well, thank goodness for small mercies. Nothing untoward in there this morning, no abandoned towels or bathing robes. Evidently her last missive on the subject had finally stopped that foul practice. She flicked the sauna switch to 'On' and set the timer. Fifteen to twenty minutes later the temperature should have reached its peak. It was time to open the gents and ladies huts and get the heat going inside there too.

Two minutes later Helle was in the middle of her disrobing ritual. Though there weren't any set places for members – claiming a space as 'your own' was another of those foul practices that was severely frowned upon – she enjoyed undressing in the little nook at the back. Not only was it right beside the radiator, there were extra hooks (very useful for hanging floor-length fur coats, fur headbands and long pashmina scarves). This was her guilty pleasure and one of the benefits of being the FVI (First Viking In – responsible for opening the club). The floor of the changing hut was wooden and cold, so she stood on a small mat while she undressed. After use the mat could be neatly rolled up, ready to be stored on the top shelf of the hut.

There were voices outside, accompanied by the sound of blowing noses and a hacking cough – some of the Oldies had arrived. Helle quickly pulled on her thick terry towelling dressing gown and put her gold watch into the bottom of her handbag, along with her set of club keys. If she hurried, she could be naked solely before the eyes of her God and not before the eyes of the club members. Not that Helle was ashamed of her body, she took great care of it. She took a deep breath and opened the door. Yes, her body was a temple.

She strutted across the boards like a peacock, head high, and focused her thoughts very carefully on recent events. The icy wind was doing its level best to attack her 'temple', but it hadn't reckoned on Helle's iron will. Mind was very definitely winning over matter. She reached the top of the bathing steps and looked down. Mr Rasmussen's demise was, naturally, distressing for the whole town. And their current Minister, Anita Bach Larsen, would, naturally, conduct a fitting memorial ceremony. The Minister was young so, naturally, Helle reasoned, Anita would no doubt be more than happy to have someone with long experience and personal knowledge of the community to assist with finding suitable hymns. Yes, Helle would ring the organist after her dip and set up a meeting. No, scratch that – she would ring the organist right after she called the Extraordinary Meeting of the Viking Committee.

But, really, thought Helle, as she carefully removed her robe, folded it in half and placed it in the wire basket. That man – God Rest His Troubled Soul! – had displayed a serious lack of consideration for his fellow bathers by choosing the Viking bathing bridge to end his days. Weren't there a plethora of other bridges up and down the coast from which to choose?

Helle descended the steps in her rubber bathing shoes and said a little prayer. Oh! And that bottle of *Gammel Dansk*? Was the man stark raving mad? Well, really, it was either that or a complete disregard for the safety of others. Club rules – sent to every member and a copy of which was clearly visible on the noticeboard – clearly and categorically stated that only plastic bottles were allowed on the bridge. Unless there was special dispensation, as was given for the Moonlight Bathe, for example. Ah, yes, the Moonlight Bathe. She must get the final numbers. Time and tide waited for no man, as Mr Rasmussen had discovered.

## CHAPTER 27

Karin called in at Netto, the discount supermarket, on her way home. She hadn't really eaten since hearing about Stig from the police, but she knew that she should force herself. She picked up a loaf of ready-sliced rye bread, a tub of prawn salad, a wedge of Brie and a punnet of cherry tomatoes. Her plan was to eat in front of the TV (something she never did), watch some reality TV (something she often did) and enjoy a beer (something she sometimes did with Stig). Followed by a long shower and then bed. Sleep would be good, if only her mind would stop racing.

She was surprised and slightly alarmed to find Johnny waiting outside her flat. She was even more surprised to see him looking freshly washed and holding out a bunch of flowers. Recently picked from the petrol station forecourt. She got off her bike and pushed it slowly up to the entrance, desperately wondering what to say.

Johnny stubbed out his Prince and threw it in the gutter. "Hi, beautiful! These are for you. You know, what with Stig and that—"

"Oh!" Karin locked her bike and desperately wondered how to react. "Um, thanks, they're – err – they're really lovely." She stood at the main doorway and hesitated with the key and her bag of shopping. Given the sub-zero temperature, it would seem rude not to invite Johnny up to her flat but, on the other hand, she wanted to be alone. She was desperate to get on the other side of the heavy wooden door as fast as possible. "That's really sweet of you, Johnny. I'd invite you in but—"

"Oh, no worries, beautiful." Johnny lit up another cigarette. "But I was thinking that maybe we could have a drink sometime?"

Karin's throat went dry. "A drink?"

He exhaled. "Yeah, up at Strandhøj. Be just like old times. Stig wouldn't want you to get lonely now, would he?"

Karin felt the tears coming. Her whole body ached and the only thing on her mind right now was a long shower. "No, I suppose he wouldn't."

"You can count on me, Karin. So, when you're ready, just come to Strandhøj—"

"Oh, Johnny, that's really kind. Really, it is. It's just that I'm really not in the mood right now."

"Well, if you change your mind," he moved a step closer, "you know where to find me. Or, you know, if anything needs fixing at *Æblegården*. I'm your man. Always keen to lend a hand!"

She put the flowers on top of her shopping bag and fumbled with the door key. "Oh, yes, right. Well thanks, Johnny. But, no, really, I'm okay. Thanks for these," she lifted up the flowers. "I'll see you at the funeral." She turned her key in the lock when she heard Johnny speak again, but this time not to her.

"What are you doing here?"

Karin turned and saw Mads locking his car door, smiling.

"Same as you are, no doubt, Johnny." Mads rubbed his hands together and turned up the collar of his coat, "Are you doing okay, Karin?"

"Yes, I'm okay." Now she was stuck. To go in or not to go in?

"Nice flowers."

"Erm, yes, Johnny brought them." She nodded in his direction, "He's been very kind."

"I just wanted to let you know that if you need anything—"

Johnny interrupted. "Yes, I was telling her the same. Can't have her sitting around moping, can we now."

Mads looked at Karin. "Okay, we'll give you some peace. Take care of yourself?"

Lea sighed. "Yes, okay, thanks Mads. And thanks again for the flowers, Johnny."

The main door was on a spring but, once inside, Karin very quietly pushed it until it locked with a click. She closed her eyes and put her head against the door.

CHAPTER 28

Helle was – like any other upstanding and God fearing citizen of Strandvig – all for law and order. But she really would have preferred the relevant authorities to be a little more discrete and not proclaim their presence to the whole town with the aid of the flashing light of a squad car. Helle shuddered. Just think of the publicity!

Today's windchill was five below zero and, thanks to gusting glacial winds, the red and white police tape was furiously trying to resist being stretched across the wooden deck. Behind it, a lone technician was slowly setting up and suiting up. Oh dear, oh dear, and they had the Moonlight Bathe coming up next week. They really must be moving on.

She walked up to the Incident Commander, who had his back turned to her. "Such a dreadful business, Commander," shouted Helle, against the wind, "and here, at the Vikings, of all places! The Incident Commander – a tall, dark, rugged type in his late 40s – switched off his phone and turned around. He slowly ran his hand through his rather long, thick brown hair and swept it away from his face. "Good morning, Mrs Brandt! The very person I wanted to talk to."

"Well, yes, Commander," she replied, preening herself, "I am the Chairman of the Vikings."

"I'll need a full list of your members, Mrs Brandt. And anyone else with key access to the club. Council staff perhaps? Tradesmen or the like?"

Helle, momentarily caught off guard by a rather exclusive, musky scent, quickly regained her composure. She looked up at him

– despite being a woman of large stature, the Commander towered over her.

"Why, no, Commander. We run a very tight ship here. Tradesmen are only allowed on to the bridge when accompanied by a member of the Committee. The only people who have keys are our club members. But surely," she said, placing her hand on her ample bosom, "you cannot suspect involvement from anyone in our club? I've had the honour of leading this club for three years and I can assure you, Commander, that we Vikings have a strict – a very strict – code of conduct."

"Mrs Brandt. Helle—" said the Commander, speaking slowly now and fixing her with his dark, steel-blue eyes, "May I call you Helle?" Helle, suddenly confused by a rather odd feeling in her knees, only managed to nod. "Wonderful. Well, Helle, I'm sure you appreciate that we'd like to eliminate your club members from our enquiries as soon as possible. So I'm going to require your full co-operation. And, please, do call me Daniel."

"Um, yes, yes, of course, Command–, um, Daniel!" she squeaked, leaning back on the railing for support, "I shall phone Mrs Lund, our club secretary, immediately."

It was at this point that Helle Brandt seemed to zoom out for a moment, and it was only thanks to a ginormous wave crashing against the bathing bridge and splashing her furry headband that she awoke from her divine reverie. The shouts in the background were not those of Heathcliff or Mr Darcy, but coming from the white-suited police technician on the other side of the red and white tape. He was huddled over a toolbox inside the storage hut and signalling to Commander Bro. The technician took his tongs, carefully extracted a hammer and deposited it into a plastic bag. Helle – in the absence of a dose of smelling salts and a maid running off to fetch the village doctor – readily accepted the offer to steady herself on Commander Bro's solid arm.

"The toolbox, Daniel?" she simpered. "Why, that belongs to Mr Bang!"

## CHAPTER 29

Bent sat on the chair and waited. He looked more like a small child rather than a septuagenarian, as he was small of stature and his short legs dangled rather than touched the floor. Daniel came in with a wad of papers under his arm and two plastic cups of coffee. He held one out to Bent. "Milk or sugar, Mr Bang?"

Bent reached out. "Neither, Commander. I like my coffee like I like my women. Strong and steamy!"

Daniel didn't comment – though there was definitely a slight flickering of his eyelids – but simply said, "Please, call me Daniel. Can I call you Bent?"

"You can call me whatever you like, Daniel. Just don't call me long distance, ha ha!"

Daniel forced a small smile and continued. "So, Bent, you know why we asked you to come in today—"

Bent sat upright in his chair. "Yes, I do! Holy Helle has landed me right in it!"

"Holy Helle? Mrs Brandt, you mean?"

"Yes, Mrs Brandt. Oh yes, she acts all 'holier than thou'. Always doing 'good works', and spends every free minute in the church. But she's just a big bossy boots and wants to interfere in everything."

Daniel could immediately see the image in his head – it all tied in very well with the Chairman of the Vikings Club he had met – but chose to ignore Bent's remark and tried to push on with the interview.

"We're just trying to establish a timeline. As you know, Stig Rasmussen seems to have fallen into the water after drinking half a bottle of *Gammel Dansk*."

"So you think it was an accident?"

"At this stage, Mr Bang, we're just trying to establish the facts."

"Then why did you take the toolbox? I heard you were at the Vikings yesterday."

"Yes, we did remove a toolbox from the storage hut yesterday—"

"I know. And I'm sure Holy Helle was delighted to identify it as mine!"

"Yes, she did identify it, Bent. We removed several items yesterday – including the toolbox. But that's just normal procedure in a situation like this where we're looking at a drowning accident or a possible suicide. All I want to do today is to ask you a few questions. Now, if we can just—"

"I've got nothing to hide, Daniel! Ask away... Lord only knows we all want this horrible business cleared up. Stig was a good friend, you know." He looked up at Daniel, suddenly changed. "Ole, one of us Oldies, who found Stig—"

"Ole Olsen..." Daniel looked down his list, "and his wife, Yrsa."

"Well, it's like this, Daniel." Bent paused and scratched his chin, unsure of how to go on. "Ole didn't want to say anything to Yrsa – it was a big shock for her you know, finding a body in the water like that. She's a real trooper, Yrsa. But, still," Bent shook his head, "it's not the kind of thing the ladies should ever see."

"No, of course not." Daniel nodded and waited for Bent to continue. Often the best information, not to mention the truth, came from letting people talk at random, at their own pace. Not from a question and answer session.

Bent leaned in closer and lowered his voice. "Well, Ole told me last night that when he pulled Stig out of the water that morning, his head was all bashed in."

Daniel looked down again at the pile of papers in front of him. "Mr Rasmussen's body was pulled out of the water on Friday morning and we're still awaiting the final autopsy reports. Right now we're trying to piece together what happened on Thursday night or the early hours of Friday morning."

Bent leaned back and watched Daniel closely. "I've seen what the water and rocks are capable of, Daniel. So has Ole. I'd put my life in that man's hands. But Ole says Stig's head was bashed in something terrible, much worse than just falling in the sea. His head had been bashed in on purpose. Probably with my hammer—"

Daniel put both his elbows on the table. "Bent, you know I can't possibly comment on that. We're still awaiting reports from the lab. And it would make my job here a lot easier if you didn't mention what Ole Olsen said. This is a small village and we don't want to scare anyone. Do we?"

Bent pulled back in his seat. "Ole knows what he saw. And I believe him. And that's why you're interested in the toolbox, isn't it?"

Daniel tried to change tact. "As I said, we're just trying to find out what happened. Maybe the toolbox is important. Maybe it isn't."

Stalemate.

"Okay, then, Daniel. Go on, what do you want to know?"

"Well, what can you tell me about it?"

Bent looked thoughtful. "There isn't really anything to tell. That toolbox has been in there since time immemorial, since the Vikings opened."

"When was that?"

"I can't remember the year. Ask Holy Helle – she's already making plans for some sort of jubilee."

"So it's been there for some years?"

"If I remember rightly, it was Ole's toolbox. Yrsa's a great one for tidying up and had tried to get rid of it at the *Vejloppemarked*."

Daniel looked confused. "The *vejlopp*—"

"We close the High Street on the first Saturday of September. It's a Strandvig tradition – been doing it for years. Everyone brings along a table or a rug to put down on the pavement. And any old jumble they want to sell. You'd be amazed at the junk that people are prepared to pay good money for. Ha ha, you should see Henrik and Kenneth – it's one of the highlights of their year!"

"Henrik and Kenneth, they would be The Frandsen brothers in the High Street?"

"Yes. All of a twitter they are. Buying up other folks' old scrap and rusty garden furniture." Bent took a noisy slurp of his coffee and scratched his head. "Where did I get to? Oh yes, well we sit there the whole day in our garden chairs and make quite a little party out of it."

"It all sounds very cosy."

"Oh, it is, Daniel, very *hyggelig* indeed. And Ellen Møller – have you met her yet? The town butcher, lovely woman. Widowed with three sons: Morten, Brian and Jacob. Jacob, the baby, he helps her out in the shop—"

Daniel knew that Bent was beginning to ramble again but, much against his better judgement, he was quite enjoying the story. Not at all like life over in Odense when the nearest he had ever come to *hygge* was being invited to speak at the Odense Neighbourhood Watch Residents Association's monthly meeting and being presented with a tin of Danish cookies for his efforts. He had tried to resist accepting the tin – personal gifts weren't strictly permitted – but as the cookies had been handmade by old Mrs Jarnvig, he hadn't the heart to turn her down. He had made amends with his conscience by sharing them with the desk officers and rationing himself to enjoying one cookie at a time.

Bent took another slurp of his coffee which now, in contrast to the ladies of his harem, was cold and murky. "Where was I? Oh, yes. Ellen, she fires up the barbecue and keeps us supplied with sausages, pork chops and potato salad. Aye, it's a grand day indeed. Though there are a few that turn their noses up at it. Martin and Maria Brix – couple of snobs, they are. And that old bear, Bertil Bruun, our bike man."

Daniel's stomach rumbled. And was inwardly screaming for Danish cookies.

Footsteps passed by in the corridor and Daniel flinched. He sat up in his chair and shuffled his papers. "So...the toolbox, Bent?"

"The toolbox? Oh, no-one wanted the toolbox, did they? And then Yrsa had the bright idea of leaving it at the Vikings. There are always little odd jobs to be done. Tap washers that need changing. New nails for the boards."

Daniel took out his Montblanc pen – a gift from his father when he entered the service – and started to write. "So the toolbox and its contents are Ole's."

"Yes and no. We've all added to it over the years. And if we needed to buy anything specific – spare parts and the like – they were bought with money from the Vikings' kitty."

Daniel stopped writing. "There's cash kept at the Vikings?"

"Oh no, no cash these days, Daniel. We did have a jar but that was years ago, in the very early days of the club. Trouble was, the local boys would break in and use the hut at night – and steal any money that was in the jar. Nothing big – just fifty *kroner* or so – but we had to stop leaving cash in there. These days it all goes through the club's bank account. Holy Helle is a mighty pain in the ass, but I'll say one thing for the woman, she's as straight as a die when it comes to the accounting. You can ask Ole."

Daniel continued writing. "So back to the toolbox. Who has access to it? And access to the club after hours?"

"Well, anyone with a key to the main gate and storage hut."

"And who has a key?"

"All the Committee members. And there's a spare key, for emergencies, which is kept on Stig's bunch at the Kro. But we saw him hanging it up behind the bar that night. Ask Lea, she was there. And I can't think for the life of me why Stig would be down at the Vikings. He said he was off home."

At least that narrowed it down. Daniel opened a file. "Yes, Mrs Brandt has already given us the list of Committee members and keys—"

Bent continued. "And, of course, there's a spare key for the storage hut underneath the brick."

"The brick?"

"Yes, under the brick. On the right-hand side of the door. I think probably everyone in the club knows about it."

Brilliant, just brilliant. Daniel sighed. "I didn't see a brick there yesterday, Bent. And we made a full search. So where's that brick now? And the key?"

Bent thought about it. "I have no idea, Daniel. Now you mention it, I don't think the brick was there on Friday morning when I was in the hut."

"You went into the hut on Friday? The day Mr Rasmussen's body was found?"

"Yes. I was looking for that old bottle of *Gammel Dansk*."

Daniel watched Bent closely. "You were looking for a bottle of *Gammel Dansk*?" Mrs Brandt had mentioned finding an empty bottle on the bathing bridge. Which he had had removed from the bin for fingerprinting.

"Not for me, Daniel. It was for Yrsa. Medicinal, you know. But I didn't find it."

"Did you touch the toolbox?"

"No, not on Friday. I used it on Thursday morning because Holy Helle was chasing me to repair the door."

"So you were in the hut on Thursday. But there was nothing unusual in the hut on Friday when you entered it. Nothing out of place? Nothing missing?"

"Nope. Just like it always is, a bit of a mess. Cold and damp and clammy."

"Do you smoke, Bent?"

Bent's eyes flickered and for a moment he was confused.

"Bent? Do you smoke?"

Bent was lost in his own thoughts for a second but then seemed to dismiss those thoughts just as quickly. He lifted up the plastic cup, and looked down inside at the cold dregs of coffee. "Me, Daniel? No, sorry, I can't help you there. Look at me – the very picture of health! Gave that nasty habit up years ago."

Daniel decided to let it go. He stood up and shook Bent's hand. "Thanks for coming in and being so helpful."

"Not at all, not at all." He looked Daniel in the eye. "I think you might just like it here, you know."

"The station?"

"Strandvig."

"I'm only here for six months, Bent."

Bent rolled up his yellow beanie. "You mark my words. In fact, I bet you 100 *kroner* that you're still here for our next *Vejloppemarked!*"

Daniel laughed. "I don't think so, Bent. Anyway, I'm not a betting man."

"No, I can see that. You look like a decent man. A girl could do worse and I know someone who might be right up your street!"

Daniel clapped Bent's shoulder as he walked towards the door. There was something incredibly endearing about the little, funny man.

Daniel snapped back to his senses. "Oh, but Bent!"

Bent turned around in the doorway. "Yes, Daniel?"

"I'd really appreciate it if you didn't share what Ole Olsen said to you."

Bent put his fingers up to his neck. "Right you are, Daniel. *Ama'r halshug.*"

101

# CHAPTER 30

"Sit down, Kenneth, and let me make you a nice cup of mocha." Henrik steered his better, smaller half towards their Børge Mogensen black leather sofa and covered his knees with a black and grey geometric print lambswool blanket.

"But, Henrik, it's just so awful! I mean, first, poor Stig is dead. And, if that isn't bad enough, the police think it's murder? Here, in Strandvig? It just doesn't make any sense. I mean, really – Stig? God rest his soul!" He buried his head in his hands, ignoring the *kransekage* Henrik was holding out.

Henrik lifted the dish to his nose and savoured the smell of marzipan. The dainty pastry logs, drizzled with white icing, were perfectly lined up on the brown, retro stoneware plate.

"Well, we don't know that for sure, *skat*. I only heard it from Ellen. Yrsa was in the butchers this morning buying a few titbits for Ole. Not surprising that he's lost his appetite since pulling Stig out of the water. And, I mean to say, who can really blame him?"

"Must have got the shock of his life!" said Kenneth, pulling his knees up underneath the rug and nursing his mocha.

"This whole business would make anyone lose their appetite," said Henrik, reaching for a second piece of *kransekage*. "'A small dish of hot liver pâté and a couple of breaded fish fillets – that should fair give him his strength back,' Ellen reckoned. Well, Yrsa said the police had been round again. Same questions as before, but they wanted specific details. Had they noticed anything strange when they opened the club on Friday? Was the padlock still on the main gate? Any blood or hair on the steps... The police said Stig had a lot of gashes on the back of his head."

"Well, of course, he did," Kenneth argued, "He must have been bashed to bits. Remember what Bent said. Stig had been in the water for hours. And you know yourself what the rocks are like down there—"

"But, *skat*," said Henrik, reaching for his third piece of *kransekage* and playing his trump card, "from what Ellen could make out, the police seem to think Stig was dead before he entered the water!"

"Oh my God, so it might be murder then?"

"Well, it's certainly looking that way. Imagine that, here in Strandvig. That'll certainly put us on the map!"

"Do we want to be on that kind of map?"

Henrik licked his finger and used it to pick up all the *kransekage* crumbs from the plate. "You know what they say, *skat*. There's no such thing as bad publicity."

"Well, I suppose so—"

"On the other hand, that means that there's a killer amongst us."

"Hmm—"

"Which means that anyone in Stig's circle is a potential suspect. Yes, the police are going to be looking under every stone. Things are definitely going to heat up around here!"

Kenneth shivered and pulled the Klippan rug right up to his nose.

# CHAPTER 31

B ent and Lea sat on the bottom bench of the sauna. Normally they would go straight for the top bench and the constant, pulsating heat. But running through the events of the last few days would require a long, slow simmer. Lea recounted the facts as she knew them. The police had questioned Bent after the removal of the hammer and toolbox, but were content with his testimony and let him go. According to Henrik, who had heard it from Ellen, who had heard it from Mrs Meyer who cleaned the police station, there were prints all over the toolbox, but none on the hammer. It had been mysteriously wiped clean. Possible murder weapon, exhibit A? The police still maintained that they were investigating a fatal accident but the hammer, together with Ole's suspicions had set the whole town talking.

Bent had no obvious motive, but did have an ironclad alibi. After waving goodnight to Lea at Strandhøj Kro, he had spent the night with a lady friend. Bent was too much of a gentleman to name names, but Lea knew it was one of the Oldest Swinger in Town's harem.

Lea went through the scenario again. "Okay, there was no sign of forced entry and every member of the Vikings has their own key. So, in theory, any one of us could have killed Stig, right?"

"But your key only opens the inside gate, sweetheart. The main gate is padlocked every night and unlocked every morning. Committee members are the only ones with those particular keys. Plus the emergency one that's kept at the Kro, on Stig's bunch."

"So who are we looking at, apart from yourself? Ole and Yrsa – they were the ones who discovered Stig, but I think we can

104

safely count them out, can't we. Then there's our beloved Chairman—"

"Holy Helle? Unlikely. Though I admit, she can be brutal when riled. But, no, I think we can rule her out, unless," grinned Bent, "she's so hard up that she's going to start knocking off villagers just for the extra church services."

"Perish the thought! Moving swiftly on... Elvira Lund, Ida's granny and club secretary? She must be 75 if she's a day and can hardly get down the bathing steps."

Bent chortled, "Elvira? Don't let the walking stick fool you. I can tell you that, for an old lass, she's in pretty good physical form."

"Oh, good lord, Bent," said Lea, putting her hands over her ears, "I don't want to know!"

"Must be the yoga. I can tell you, that woman can get into all sorts of positions—"

"Bent, please! I'll never be able to look Elvira in the eye again!"

"Might want to take up yoga, yourself, sweetheart. Good for the body. And the mind." He pointed at the bruise on her thigh and winked. "Or maybe you've been up to some yoga yourself lately?" He let his question hang in the air.

"What do you mean, Bent?"

"I thought maybe you and Mads—"

Lea looked straight out the window. "Well, you thought wrong, Bent. Mads is ancient history."

Bent whistled. "I saw him with a bunch of flowers on Friday. They weren't for you?"

"I told him where to stick them. A leopard doesn't change his spots, Bent."

Bent whistled. "You've certainly changed your spots recently, Lea Mus. From a quiet little mouse to a fighting tiger!"

Lea laughed. "Yes, this year is going to be different, Bent. No more Lea Mus! The quiet little *mus* has to go!"

"I'm not sure if I can handle that, Lea Mus. Begging your pardon, I mean, Lea!" He winked. "Anyway, our Mads used to have a key when he lived here. But it couldn't be him, of course."

"No, of course not. He's just moved back here." Should she tell Bent about the Kayak Club? But she couldn't tell him that Mads wasn't home that night because then Bent, in turn, would ask her what she had been doing there. Knocking on Mads' door in the middle of the night. "Um, so who else?"

Bent looked out the sauna windows and focused on the horizon. The sky was dark grey this morning, the sea midnight blue and calm. "Kenneth has a padlock key, too. But I can't remember the last time he opened or closed the club. He's always so busy with the shop. You'd think that Helle would be reading him the riot act, but she lets him off because he's so generous with sponsorship."

Lea flinched.

"What's up, Lea Mus? Surprised that Holy Helle isn't so holy after all?" grinned Bent. "We all have our little secrets…"

Lea wasn't sure what to say or where to start. "Bent, when we were at Strandhøj on Thursday night, I saw Kenneth in the corridor talking to Stig. It was all very secretive."

"Stig? Talking to Kenneth?"

"I know. Crazy, isn't it. They were in the corridor, and Kenneth was handing over a load of money. I couldn't hear what they were talking about… Something or other about Stig promising to keep Kenneth's 'secret safe'."

"Are you sure, Lea Mus?"

"Of course, it could all be completely harmless," Lea went on quickly, more in an attempt to convince herself than Bent. "I mean, Kenneth and Henrik are devoted to each other. Right?"

CHAPTER 32

Commander Bro ushered her in. "Thanks for coming in today, Lea. We're talking to everyone who was at Strandhøj Kro that night. Just trying to establish a timeline, there's nothing to fear."

"Of course." She sat down and tried not to look at him directly. But tried not to avoid his gaze either. Wow, did policemen normally look this good? Bent hadn't been kidding.

"And you're a Viking, too?" he said, looking at the list in front of him and then directly at her. Lea could feel a queasy sensation at the bottom of her stomach, her forehead was freezing. "I was a winter bather myself in Odense, before I transferred here. I'm tempted to get back in the water. But no doubt the Vikings have a pretty long waiting list?"

Lea tried, and failed miserably, to focus. She wondered what he looked like in a towel. Only a towel. With that mop of hair, he probably had a really hairy chest. She made a note to self: shave legs at earliest opportunity. The cold feeling in her head was being challenged by a heat rising from her cheeks.

"So, Lea. Just to go over things again. At what time, approximately, did Mads Sørensen leave Strandhøj Kro?"

"Mads? What's he got to do with his? He doesn't even have a key to the Vikings. Not any more—"

"We're just trying to piece together who saw Stig Rasmussen last. That's all. Do you know what time Mr Sørensen left?"

Lea tried to breathe calmly. "Um, the back of ten, I think. I was with some friends – perhaps they can be more specific."

107

Daniel looked down at his notes. "That would be Bent Bang, Kenneth and Henrik…the Frandsen brothers?"

"Um, yes, that's them." Lea was stopped in her tracks for a second. Wow, even the police didn't seem to know what Henrik's real surname was.

"And Mads was alone? You're quite sure about that."

"Yes. He left by the side door – that's the one that leads straight to Strandhøj car park. He said he was heading to the Kayak Club, that's where he's living right now."

"Okay, thanks. And there was nothing unusual in Mads Sørensen's behaviour that night?"

"No, nothing I can think of." Lea wriggled in her seat. Why was it so hot in there?

"Nothing he did." Daniel looked at her directly. "Or said to you, perhaps?"

God, but he was persistent. "Um, no. We only chatted very briefly."

"About anything in particular?"

"Mads has just moved back to Strandvig. He just wanted to say 'hi'."

"So Mads is an old friend then?"

Lea's eyes moved to the clock behind Daniel's desk. "Erm, yes. An old friend."

He sat back in his chair and observed her carefully. "I see. And that was the last you saw of Mads Sørensen that night?"

"Um, yes, that's right." Which was true. She hadn't lied, she hadn't seen him again. But then again, she hadn't mentioned that Mads hadn't been at the Kayak Club when she called… Oh my God, please let me get out of here before I crack.

"I see. Okay. Well, great, thanks for coming in, Lea," he said, standing up and coming over to help her out of her chair. Lea fumbled with her coat and bag and took an awkward step backwards. Daniel put out a hand to steady her. "Here, this is my card. The first number is my mobile. If you remember anything else

108

you can call me," he said, placing an arm on her shoulder, "day or night, Lea."

Lea took the card and rolled her coat and handbag into a ball and exited the room as fast as she could without breaking out into a full sprint. Halfway down the corridor, she could still feel Daniel's eyes on the back of her neck. And her back. And her backside. Yes, definitely her backside.

CHAPTER 33

Why does he never answer his bloody phone? Lea tried calling Bent's number again. She tried not to imagine what he was probably doing right at this minute. It probably involved a strange position and one – or could that be several – of his harem. Focus, Lea! The call went straight to Bent's answerphone. Yet again. "Well hullo there, ladies! You've come to the right place! Bent Bang at your service. I'm busy right now, but leave a message and—"

Lea decided to leave a message this time. "Hi Bent, it's Lea. Listen, I've just had a call from Kenneth. He's frantic and wants to meet me. And I had to swear not to say a word to Henrik. Do you think it's about him and Stig? Anyway, I'm off to the Kro right now. Call me when you can!"

## CHAPTER 34

Lea and Kenneth sat by the window, with a large platter of Danish charcuterie and cheese in front of them. It was pitch black outside and the candles made a beautiful reflection in the window.

"Thanks for meeting me, Lea," said Kenneth, knocking back yet another glass of Amarone. Lea couldn't quite see because of the candlelight, but it looked like Henrik's tongue was beginning to turn purple. Yet another good reason to stick to white, she thought, taking a piece of freshly baked bread from the basket, and coating it with a thick layer of butter.

"That's okay, Kenneth. What's up?" She took a bite and looked down at the bread. "My God, this is good. Are you sure you don't want a piece before I eat the whole lot?"

"Oh, no – I couldn't. Really, I can't eat a morsel right now. You see, I've been so worried. I don't think I can keep this secret anymore—"

He stopped talking when Johnny suddenly appeared behind Lea's chair. "Hi, folks – well, well, well, this all looks very cosy! Does Henrik know what you're up to, Kenneth? I can keep a secret!"

Kenneth looked horrified and could only manage a squawk in return.

"Don't worry, Kenneth, another glass of Amarone and another basket of bread, right? And for you, beautiful? Your usual white?"

"Thanks, Johnny, that would be lovely."

Johnny leaned over the table and replaced their candles. "To be honest, Lea, I'm a bit surprised to see you here with Kenneth.

Didn't think he was your type. You're still running after Mads, aren't you?"

Lea, completely caught off guard, stared at him in disbelief.

Kenneth managed to loosen the grip on his wine glass and found his voice. "Johnny, do leave poor Lea alone! You know fine well that that was a long time ago. Please don't start digging up all that old business, will you? I couldn't bear it. They've both moved on. Haven't you, Lea? So just leave—"

"Righty-oh, then. I'll leave you two alone. To your secrets..." He winked at Lea. "And I'll be right back with more hot bread!"

Lea sighed. "Okay, Kenneth, spit it out. What's all this about? I can't stand the suspense any longer. And make it quick, before Johnny comes back and pokes his big nose in. Talking of which, why isn't Ida serving tonight?"

Kenneth took a fortifying sip of his wine. "Ida left not two minutes before you came in. Maria Brix phoned here and spoke to Karsten – because Ida wasn't answering her phone – saying she needed Ida immediately. Some kind of emergency at the Brix household."

"Let me guess. Maria has run out of organic tea bags?"

Kenneth winked. "Oh my, you're getting so naughty, Lea! Anyway, getting back to my own emergency... Remember last Thursday—"

"How could I not? That was the last time we saw Stig—"

Kenneth took another swig. "I have a little confession to make—"

The front door opened and the noise level in the Kro dropped immediately. Lea, Kenneth and the other patrons looked round. It was like a scene from a western movie: there was most definitely a stranger in town... It was the Sheriff.

## CHAPTER 35

Daniel Bro took a quick look around the room. Not because he expected to know anyone in there – it was more an attempt on his behalf to get his bearings and try to 'blend in'. Not something he was particularly good at. He wouldn't be staying long (three litres of full-fat milk, a large foil container of liver pâté, a kilo jar of Nutella – bought by his mother for him at a German border shop – and a loaf of organic ryebread were waiting back at his lodgings), so he removed *Kystbladet* from the magazine rack and sat down on one of the bar stools. Perched on the side, more than sat, his legs longer than those of the average pub punter.

"Oh, good evening Commander Bro! Here to make an arrest are you? Any news?"

Daniel looked around. "I'm off duty actually, Mr Holm."

"Call me Karsten. Well, well, well, how nice of you to call in. May I formally welcome you on behalf of the wife, Lisbeth here, and myself – *Mein Host* – to Strandhøj Kro?"

Karsten was on top form tonight, having just been shown the accounts by Lisbeth. Last year's takings were the highest ever. And they hadn't even had the final figures for December. The Christmas season had been especially hard work this time with back-to-back lunches, but it would all be worth it when they were lying on the beach in Phuket at the start of February: two weeks in Thailand, their main holiday of the year.

Lisbeth beamed and almost curtsied at the sight of the Commander, who was almost double her height. "And what can we get you, Commander, this one's on us?"

"Oh, um, right," said Daniel. Not entirely at ease with the idea of accepting a free drink (or a free anything, for that matter) but, on the other hand, he was keen not to alienate the local community. Something he had learned the hard way in Odense. "That's very kind of you both, thanks. I think I'll take a *Carlsberg*."

"Coming right up! How are you liking it here?"

"Thanks," said Daniel, taking his glass of lager and lifting it at Lisbeth, then Karsten, "and *skål*! Well, it's a bit of a change from Odense – much quieter. But I love being by the sea. Strandvig seems like a good place to live. In fact," he said, looking around the room, "I was thinking that it might be a good base."

"Oh," said Lisbeth, excitedly, "are you thinking of buying a flat here?"

"Renting, not buying. Not sure where I'll be in six months' time."

"Oh, because of your girlfriend? Or wife?" said Lisbeth, fishing.

Daniel patted the back of his hair. "Erm, no. No girlfriend or wife."

"Reeeeeally!" said Lisbeth, a bit too excitedly. "Oh, well you could have knocked me down with a feather! That's a surprise, isn't it, Karsten." She looked Daniel up and down, "We were sure a good-looking man like yourself would have no end of offers…"

"Well, I don't really work regular hours and—"

"I'm sure we can introduce you to some nice local girls. Can't we Karsten?"

Karsten winked. "Oh, yes. Plenty of 'hungry' ladies around these parts!"

Daniel made a mental note to avoid the front row bar seats when he came back. If he ever came back.

Lisbeth was called away to a large table of diners – regulars from the Old Boys' Badminton league. "Oh, will you excuse me, please, Commander. Ida had to leave so we're a bit short staffed. Plenty of hungry gents around these parts too!" She walked off, all chirpy, notepad in hand, ready to take orders for tonight's speciality dish of *skibberlabskovs*. Beef, onion and potatoes gently boiled together with bay leaves and black pepper. Served with thick slices of dark ryebread, butter, diced pickled beetroot and sharp mustard.

Daniel, in an attempt to divert attention from his private life, tried a new tack. "Are you from Strandvig, Karsten?"

"Oh, yes, yes, Commander. I was born here, our family goes back generations. But Lisbeth," he said, waving over to her, "well, she's from Aarhus." Karsten lowered his voice and leaned over the bar towards Daniel. "Want to hear a joke?"

Daniel, who was beginning to get hungry, nodded and picked up a menu. The smell of black pepper emanating from the *skibberlabskovs* was starting to tickle his nose. Not entirely unpleasant.

"You're going to love this one! Two robbers from Aarhus are being chased by the police..."

Daniel momentarily raised his eyebrows, but quietly sipped his pint and gestured for Karsten to continue.

"The police are starting to gain on them. So Karl says, 'Quick, in here!' and they take a detour into the local sports stadium—"

Karsten was momentarily interrupted by Johnny, asking for a glass of Amarone. "Another one for Kenneth? My, but he's in a right tizzy tonight. What's got into him?" Daniel turned around on the stool and spotted Kenneth, who – having failed to physically hide under the table for two – was doing his utmost to hide behind the empty basket of bread. Daniel also spotted Lea and made an awkward half-salute, half-wave in her direction. Lea nodded and Kenneth continued to cower – too frightened to move. Daniel swivelled back to the bar and smoothed down the back of his hair. The Carlsberg seemed to be making a huge, echoing hole in the bottom of his stomach so, dismissing all thoughts of the cold liver pâté waiting for him back at his digs, he asked for a plate of *skibberlabskovs*.

Karsten beamed, "Excellent choice!" He scratched his head. "So where was I, Commander? Oh, yeah. So they're running around the athletics track and Karl is going like the clappers. Like Wilson Kipketer – but pale white and wobbly." Daniel cringed inwardly. "Karl turns around and sees his mate, Dennis, lagging behind. 'Hurry up, Dennis!' he shouts. The police are right behind you!"

"Uh huh," said Daniel, holding his pint to his lips and praying that the end was near.

"And Dennis shouts back, 'Don't worry, Karl. They're three laps behind!'"

Daniel sincerely hoped the *skibberlabskovs* would be more palatable.

## CHAPTER 36

The Amarone was beginning to work its magic on Kenneth's nerves. It would, of course, have made for a much cheaper evening all round if he had grasped the thistle by the root and ordered a full bottle from the off. But Kenneth – now on glass number four – wasn't caring and neither was *Mein Host* Karsten.

Lea's cheeks were just as flushed as Kenneth's. She had limited herself – as she always did on weeknights – to two glasses of white. Watered down with as much water as her bladder could tolerate. Why did she have a child's bladder? But the arrival of Commander Bro, together with Kenneth's bizarre behaviour made her feel guilty. So her body reacted as it always did in such situations. Cue the flush. And there she was, as innocent as the proverbial lamb.

"Kenneth, come up from behind that basket? What on earth are you doing?"

"Oh, Lea! Commander Bro is here. He must be on to me!"

"He is?" She turned around and sneaked another look at Daniel. Sitting there with his long legs and his thick dark hair, maybe he was actually rather–

"Oh, Lea! I've got a confession to make…"

Lea gulped. As much as she was dying to know exactly what had gone on in the corridor between Kenneth and Stig that fatal night, she really wasn't ready to hear that her friend was in any way involved in Stig's death. Accidental or not.

"I had a meeting with Stig on the night he was killed."

"Go on." There was no need to let Kenneth know what she had witnessed.

"It was driving me crazy, trying to keep it from Henrik. You know how suspicious he is – a real Sherlock Holmes!"

A rather portly Sherlock Holmes, thought Lea. "Yes, yes. Go on!"

"Well, I wanted to set up something special for Henrik's birthday—"

"His birthday?!"

"Yes, his birthday."

Lea sat back with a slump. It certainly wasn't the kind of secret rendezvous between Stig and Kenneth that she had concocted in her head. But then why was Henrik handing over money—

"…round one." Kenneth peered at her. "Are you listening, Lea?"

Henrik was round, portly… Lea looked puzzled.

"His birthday, Lea! It's a 'round' one. A milestone."

"Oh, yes, of course, right." She lifted up her wine glass.

Kenneth sipped and continued. "He'll be fifty."

"Fifty?!" She managed not to spit out her wine. More like fifty-five or sixty. Though any tangible proof, like Henrik's birth certificate, had probably been burnt many moons ago.

Kenneth held his glass in mid-air and fixed her with his eyes. "Yes, Lea. Fifty."

"Oh, yes, of course. Fifty it is then." She sneaked a look at Daniel who seemed to be in Karsten's comedy clutches. She was sure she wasn't imagining it – Daniel definitely seemed to be interested. Something in the way he looked at her. Or didn't look at her. But what about Mads, Lea? Mads Sørensen could go take a hike! And take his stupid bunch of petrol station flowers with him. Daniel had given her his card, now where exactly had she put it?

"Is he watching me?"

"Who?"

"Commander Bro?!"

118

"Oh, no, you're fine. I was just checking. Go on…"

"I thought it would be fun to throw Henrik a huge surprise party."

"Uh huh." Lea couldn't help thinking that the very idea of Henrik turning 50 would be a surprise for the whole village. You could see he was dyeing his hair a mile off… "But where does Stig come in?"

"He said he'd fix it with Karsten that we'd have a little party here right after the Moonlight Bathe."

"So that's why you were handing him a lot of cash, then?"

"How do you know about that?" Kenneth shot another glance at Daniel, but was relieved to see that he was happily downing his first plate of *skibberlabskovs*.

"I was in the ladies toilets and, erm, happened to see you."

"What? Does anyone else know? Who have you told?"

"Relax, Kenneth! Not a soul." Bent didn't count, did he? "But then Karsten must know? And Lisbeth and Johnny and—"

"No. You're the only one. Stig was going to speak to Karsten about the party on Friday morning, before Johnny and the others arrived. It was to be top secret."

"But why all the money?" She believed Kenneth and it sounded plausible, it really did. (Just not the 'Henrik turns fifty' part.) But weren't murderers always described by their neighbours as being "a really nice bloke, never had any trouble from him, kept himself to himself"? Lea wanted to be sure.

"Well, I gave Stig the money, because he was going to be ordering the *hors d'oeuvres* for the party. They're coming from that wonderful Spanish tapas bar in the city. *Mi casa, su casa*. Do you know it? Lovely little place. Rustic. They do the most wonderful *albóndigas* and Henrik is just crazy about their spicy *mejillones* and *patatas bravas*—"

Lea speared a piece of cheese from the platter in front of them. "So have you told Commander Bro?"

"Have you gone mad, Lea? Of course not! If he finds out, he'll put two and two together and get five!"

Lea wasn't so sure, to her Commander Bro looked pretty competent. And he had such a lovely thick head of hair. She grabbed another piece of bread. "According to what I read, when they found Stig, all he had on him was his wallet. No keys, no phone. And the wallet was empty. Bank cards but no mention of cash—"

"I know, Lea! I read the same thing in *Kystbladet*."

"So whoever killed Stig must have pocketed all that money?"

Kenneth nodded. He was sad about losing the money, but was prepared to sacrifice the loss in exchange for being kept out of police enquiries and having desk lamps shone in his face.

Johnny popped up from nowhere and beamed. "More bread! And another glass for you Kenneth. Karsten says this one's on the house."

"Oh, I say, that's very kind." Kenneth raised his glass and waved over at Karsten.

"You're looking very dapper, Johnny. Hot date tonight?"

Johnny spied Karin coming in through the side door of the Kro and winked. "Maybe I have and maybe I haven't, Lea."

Lea turned around and followed his gaze. "Karin?"

"Sssh! Keep your voice down – and stop looking, will you?" Johnny was hopping from one foot to the other and trying to smooth down his hair, with little success despite his best efforts.

"Is Karin here to meet you?" Lea was astonished to see Karin out and about. Never mind out on a 'hot date' with Johnny.

"I've been round to see her a few times. Told her that I'm here for her."

"Well, I never saw that coming. Good for you, Johnny! Go to her!" Kenneth was lying through his teeth. He didn't see any future for Johnny and Karin as a pair. Stig had been Karin's soul mate and he couldn't see any man – least of all Johnny – fulfilling that role. Whether platonic or romantic. But Kenneth was pleased to see Karin come out of hiding. And pleased about this unexpected diversion that would surely remove Johnny from their immediate vicinity.

Johnny preened himself, his confidence rising by the second. "Well, Lea, I'm just like your Mads. I like to keep them guessing—"

Lea, lacking Kenneth's intake of alcohol and apparent benevolence, was beginning to see red. "Johnny, for the last time, he is not 'my Mads'!"

Johnny nodded over towards the door. "Oh really? Talk of the devil and he's sure to appear!" Lea turned around in her seat and craned her neck. Mads was standing in the doorway, waving over at them. Oh, please God, not again.

"If it ain't lover boy now!"

## CHAPTER 37

Karin stood on the mat, stamped her feet and tried to get the feeling back into her toes. She pulled back the furry hood of her purple goose-down coat and shook her hair loose, taking a furtive look behind her, but there was no-one there. All the noise was coming from within. She pulled off her thermal gloves and gave her hair a quick fluff up with her fingers. The ends of her hair were still slightly damp: she really should have used the hairdryer after her shower. She took one last deep breath and opened the door of the Kro. And was almost caught off guard by an unexpected blast of dry heat coming from the little fan above the doorway.

Karsten looked up and smiled as she walked in. She hesitated for a moment, but decided that she really didn't want to sit right there at the bar. First off, she knew his jokes too well and secondly, she'd much rather be on her own. To be honest, she would much rather be on her own at home.

Karin looked around the room, trying not to focus on anyone in particular. Damn, he wasn't here yet. She resisted the urge to look at her watch and decided to cut her losses and sit down at the first free table, one of the tables closest to the bar. It had been such a long time since she had been at Strandhøj. She thought about the last time she had been in here just a couple of weeks ago. It had been with Stig, of course. Come to think of it, had she ever been in the Kro without him? This is where they came under-age drinking together. Where they had been on their first real date together. And for the past ten years (or was it twenty?), she had been sitting at the bar alongside him, or watching him work on the other side of it. Her stomach somersaulted. Yet here she was. Standing at a table. Meeting someone else. It all felt…wrong.

She felt so guilty. Everyone from Strandvig had been so kind after what had happened, everyone had rallied round. But the attention had almost been too much, too intrusive. Karin looked after others: they weren't supposed to look after her. She struggled to pull the chair out from under the table and was convinced that every eye in the Kro was watching her every, awkward move.

She sat down and moved the candles and vase into the very centre of the table. Then did the same with the salt and pepper mills, lining them up neatly. Took off her purple coat, folded her tartan scarf very carefully, paired her gloves together and placed them inside her handbag. All those years working with toddlers had resulted in an instinctive habit of putting things away when they were no longer in use. A place for everything and everything in its place. And here, on her own, she felt very much out of place. She checked her watch and tried to slow down her breathing, keeping her thermal winter boots very firmly on the floor. She had just finally made the decision to stand up and go over to the bar and order a drink when Johnny and Mads appeared before her simultaneously, as if by magic.

Johnny was grinning like a Cheshire cat and standing to attention like the proverbial soldier. If it hadn't been so noisy in the Kro, you could have heard the clicking of his heels. "Hi, beautiful! Well, well, well – and here was me thinking you were trying to avoid me! Let me just serve a couple of customers and then I'm all yours. Now, lovely lady, what can I get you? A gin and tonic, that's your usual, isn't—"

Mads took off his black leather jacket, threw it down on the chair next to Karin, bent over and gave her a big peck on the cheek. "Hi Karin! So sorry I'm late."

Karin didn't get the chance to get a single word out.

Johnny leaned back and held his tray in front of him, like a shield. "Are you here with Mads?"

"Oh, erm. Mads thought it would be good for me to get out. You know, after what happened…"

"Oh, right." For once, Johnny was lost for an answer. "I see."

Mads smiled and rubbed Karin's arm. "Can't have Karin sitting all alone at home, can we now Johnny? Stig wouldn't have wanted that."

"No. No, we can't. I told her the same thing myself." He looked at Karin. "Didn't I Karin?"

Karin felt the urge to bolt straight for home, back to the safety of the four walls and silence of her flat. She made a move to stand up. "I was just about to order at the bar—"

Mads stopped her. "Just you sit tight. I'll get this – tonight is my treat." He looked up at Johnny. "You'll sort us out, won't you, Johnny? Bottle of white wine and two glasses, please. Oh, and make sure it's really well chilled will you?"

Johnny looked from Mads to Karin, who was rooted to her chair, sick with shame. "Thanks ever so much, Johnny. That's really sweet of you. You were always such a big help to Stig. Always keen to lend a hand."

Johnny turned on his heels and went through the swing door into the kitchen, tray hanging down by his side.

## CHAPTER 38

Lea sat straight in her chair, eyes firmly planted on Kenneth, who was caressing his glass of Amarone.

"Lea, don't pay any attention to Johnny. But look, you can tell me. Is there anything going on between you and Mads?"

"God, Kenneth, I'm so confused. You know very well that I don't want to get involved with Mads. You saw what happened last time. It wasn't pretty."

"God, yes. But? I know there's a 'but' coming...!"

Lea closed her eyes. "But there's just something about Mads that I can't shake off. Last Thursday night, the night Stig was killed, I almost ended up—"

But Kenneth wasn't listening, he was too busy looking behind Lea's head. Eyes almost popping out of his own head.

"Oh, Kenneth, what is it now? Is it Commander Bro again? Because, to be honest, I think he's actually looking at me not you. Another one who's been sending me mixed messages." She laughed. "How absurd. Mads and Daniel Bro. No buses for years and then two come along at the same time! *Skål!*"

Kenneth wasn't laughing. Or drinking. "Lea, I think you had better look for yourself. Karin isn't here for a hot date with our Johnny. She's here with Mads."

## CHAPTER 39

Karsten caught her as she was leaving. "Hey Lea, do you know where Mads is?"

Lea scowled. "How would I know? Why don't you try asking Karin? He's here with her." What was up with everyone tonight?

"No need to bite my nose off, love! Talking of noses—"

"Goodnight, Karsten!" She tried her best to slam the door behind her but, as it was a self-closing swing hinge, the effect was rather less dramatic than she had hoped.

Karsten looked back at the others sitting at the bar. He really didn't care who his audience was – just as long as he had one. And Daniel, who had also watched Lea leave, still had his head up and appeared to be listening. "So, talking of noses… Do you know why the people of Aarhus have such big noses?"

Daniel pushed the empty plate away from him. He was feeling mellow after the *skibberlabskovs*. Relaxed and beginning to quite enjoy himself. "I'm not sure—"

"Because they have such big fingers! Ha ha, I thought a bright policeman like you would have figured that one out!"

Mads appeared at the bar, jacket in hand and slightly out of breath. "Karsten, do you know if Lea left?"

"There you are, Mads! Yeah, a few seconds ago. You just missed her. Which is probably just as well because she was in a right mood, I can tell you—"

"Thanks!" Mads dashed towards the exit.

"Hey, come back, Mads! I need to talk to you about the Moonlight Bathe!"

Daniel looked on attentively. He finished the last of his beer and patted the back of his hair. "So tell me, Karsten. What's going on with that pair?"

Karsten looked towards the door. "Mads and Lea, you mean? Oh, they're old friends."

Daniel looked at him inquiringly. "Just old friends?"

"Well here's the thing, Commander," said Karsten, leaning in and winking, "between you and me, I really don't think they quite know themselves."

## CHAPTER 40

Mads ran to catch up with Lea, who was hotfooting it over to her bike. "Hey, Lea! Wait up! How about a nightcap, I've got a bottle of white wine chilling in the fridge."

Lea stopped, dumbfounded. "Are you serious?"

He reached out to put his arms around her, "With you, Lea, I'm always serious."

"And Karin?"

"Karin? Karin's a good friend."

Lea started to move away.

Mads laughed. "Oh, Lea, surely you don't think me and Karin..?"

Lea didn't know what to believe, she was hurt and annoyed. She shook him off. "Mads, I went to the Kayak Club and you weren't there."

"What?"

"The night Stig died."

"What are you on about?"

"You invited me round, remember? For a glass of chilled white wine, you said. 'You know where to find me, Lea. Day or night, Lea'", she added, imitating him. "So I came by. And you know what, I rang the doorbell and you weren't there."

"Yes, I was."

"No, you weren't!" By now she was angry. "Do you want to tell me where you really were that night? Because I can go right back into the bar and speak to my good friend, Commander Bro." Now she had his attention. "And he can take you down to the station for questioning!" she added childishly.

He backed away and shrugged, "Well, I must have gone to bed and didn't hear it."

Lea gave up. "Mads, you know what? I don't care. No more stupid flowers. Just leave me alone from now on. Okay?"

# CHAPTER 41

Lea turned down the radio and answered her phone. Almost knocking over her coffee cup in the process. "Godmorgen, Lea Mus!"

Why on earth was Bent calling her this early? "*Godmorgen,* Bent! What's up? I'm just on my way to the Vikings now——"

"I thought you would want to know." Bent sounded worried. "The police have taken Mads in for questioning."

## CHAPTER 42

Bent and Lea sat in the sauna. Lea had been in the water three times in a row in an attempt to calm her galloping brain, but it hadn't had the desired effect. She felt like an overwound clock. She took a swig of water, then made a series of stripes in the condensation on the outside of the plastic bottle with her index finger. "But, Bent, why on earth would the police suspect Mads?"

"Seems they got an anonymous tip. A phone call."

"How do you know that?"

"Do you know Mrs Meyer?"

"Ellen's friend, the cleaner? The one who cleans the police station?" Lea knew where this was leading. "Oh my God, Bent. You're not sleeping with her too, are you?"

"Oh, I didn't hear it from her, Lea Mus. I heard it from one of her friends." He winked.

"Okay, no names then. But Mads? He can't be involved!"

"I don't like it either, Lea Mus. But look at it from the point of view of the police. Mads seems to be the last one to have seen Stig on Thursday night."

"I know. But that doesn't mean he killed him. They were friends. It just doesn't make sense!"

"All I know is that Mads has been taken in to the local station." He looked dejected. "Mads is a good lad. I'm sure he has nothing to fear. You'll see."

Lea rubbed her face with her towel, then leaned forward and pressed the bottle to her forehead. She felt sick to the bottom of her stomach.

# CHAPTER 43

Lea had just left her office and was rooting around in her bag for her bike keys and lights when she saw Mads speeding towards her across the council car park. Her heart began to race. What should have been a very productive, long day (the council was open until 6 pm on Thursdays), had instead turned into a marathon session of frantic texts from Kenneth, misspelled (and incomplete) messages from Bent and – worst of all – yet another cupcake reminder from Holy Helle. And now here he was, the man of the moment. Should she be relieved or afraid?

"I was down at the station today, at the invitation of your..." Mads stopped and changed track. "At the invitation of Daniel Bro."

Lea looked up at him. "Mads, I swear to you, I had nothing to do—"

"It's okay, I know you didn't. I just... I just wanted to come and tell you first, because I know the whole town must be talking about me. I'm sorry, Lea. I'm really sorry for all this...mess."

Lea desperately tried to appear calm, but all she wanted to do was apologise to him, flinging herself straight into his arms. Why did Mads still have this effect on her? She should be kicking him in the shins. "So what happened? Why did they take you in?"

"Someone had called the station. A man. Someone trying to stitch me up."

"And?"

"They let me go. My alibi checked out and I'm cleared."

Lea was silent.

"You don't look convinced?"

"Mads, you don't have an alibi."

He spoke very slowly. "Lea, I just told you that I do. The police checked it out and you're just going to have to believe me. You don't honestly think that I could murder Stig?"

Lea didn't know what she thought. She felt sick. "That Thursday night, Mads. Where were you? I came by and you didn't answer the doorbell."

Mads looked away. "I told you, I must have fallen asleep. I'm sorry. But that's all over now and I hope that we can—"

"Mads, the Volvo wasn't there."

He rubbed the back of his head. "Oh shit."

Ha, now she had finally got him, the bloody liar. "Well, Mads?"

"Okay, listen to me. I really didn't want to get into this, but you've given me no choice. Pernille phoned and said—"

Lea felt like a bomb had exploded.

Mads tried to put his hand on her arm. "She asked me to come to Copenhagen—"

Lea felt sick to the bottom of her stomach. She turned her back on him, kicked the kickstand on her bike and started to walk away.

"Lea, please, wait. I can explain!'"

"Mads, you know what. I really couldn't give a damn!" She stormed off before the tears could start. God, she was such a fool.

CHAPTER 44

"So we're all suspects now?" Kenneth was horrified. He thought he'd successfully avoided any unpleasant questioning from the police and now his personal nightmare was beginning again.

Henrik waved out the window to Mrs Meyer, who had just left the shop and was making her way down Strandvig High Street with a Frandsen Brothers Irish linen shopping bag. Two minutes earlier Henrik had filled the bag with two packages. A stylish Stelton sink caddy, a gift from Mrs Meyer to her eldest son, who had just moved into a flat with his girlfriend. And a dainty white and silver package of luxury 'Raspberry Red' almonds from Summerbird – Mrs Meyer's favourites. A small gift from Henrik in exchange for information received on the latest events at Strandvig police station.

Henrik walked over to the coffee machine and made them both a latte. "You heard what she said, *skat*. Lisbeth got in touch with the police yesterday afternoon when she discovered that one of the sets of keys they keep behind the bar reappeared. Stig's set. Including the one with the padlock key for the Vikings."

"But I still don't see what that has to do with us?"

Henrik artfully stacked three almond cantuccini biscuits on each saucer, and topped the steaming coffees with a light sprinkling of cinnamon. "The keys weren't there on Friday morning, the police checked everything. And when they found Stig – God Rest his Soul! – he didn't have anything on him. Just an empty wallet."

Kenneth gulped.

Henrik held out the latte to Kenneth. "And now the keys are back, wiped clean of fingerprints. So someone must have put them there. The murderer."

Kenneth started to shake. "But anyone who's been at the Kro could have sneaked them back."

Henrik put his arm around him and gave him a squeeze. "Exactly, *skat*. But we don't have anything to hide, do we?"

CHAPTER 45

"What's up, Lea Mus?" Bent answered the telephone, panting.

"You've no doubt already heard on the Strandvig jungle drums about the keys?"

"Hmmmm."

"And that the police have let Mads go." Lea opened the fridge and peered inside.

More panting from Bent. "I know, it's great news!"

"Is it, Bent? He's been lying to me. Again!" Lea looked at each shelf, then rechecked the door. She had bought some white wine the other day. It had to be here somewhere.

"Oh, I'm sorry to hear that. But—" Bent started giggling. Accompanied by female tittering in the background.

Lea held the phone away from her. "Am I disturbing you?"

"I'm in the middle of a…yoga class, Lea Mus."

Eew. "Okay, give me a call later, will you?" What had she done with the bottle? Probably still in her canvas shopping bag.

"Tell you what, Lea Mus. I'll come round—" – more giggling – "to your place first thing tomorrow. I've got a few ideas about Stig's keys, but I need to ask a couple of questions first."

"Okay. But take care will you?" God, she needed that drink. It'd be lukewarm but she'd add ice. Did she have ice cubes?

"Take care? I've been doing yoga for years, Lea Mus. I can get my body into positions you wouldn't—"

Ugh. "Bent, I mean take care out…there."

"Out where, Lea Mus?"

"Out…there. You know. Strandvig."

136

# CHAPTER 46

Gustav was busy carting crates full of Coke and Faxe Kondi bottles into the back of the restaurant, when Bent arrived at Strandhøj. He parked his bike and shouted over. "Hi Gustav, can I have a quick word?"

Gustav was oblivious: lost in his music. *"Hun danser hele natten, ma chérie Bon Bon"*.

Bent prodded his arm.

Gustav removed the earbuds from his ears. "God, Bent, you gave me a fright."

"I didn't know you could sing in French. Maybe you could teach me? The ladies would like it!"

Gustav smiled and dusted the snow off the front of his parka. "The song? No, it's The Minds of 99, and they're Danish. So what's up?"

"I take it you've heard the latest – about the return of Stig's keys?"

"These ones, you mean?" Gustav held up a large bunch. "I've just been locking up out here. What about them? They hang on a hook behind the bar, anyone could have taken them, or replaced them. Including you, Bent."

Bent nodded. "Including me, sonny. But Kenneth said the police are questioning everyone again about what happened that Thursday night, every single detail, big or small. You were late that night, Karsten said so. And when I arrived, I saw you and Stig having an argument – right here in the car park. Mind telling me what it was about?"

137

Gustav looked around aimlessly, "It was nothing, Bent." He started to kick off pieces of ice that had formed on the paving stones with the heel of his boot. "Honestly."

"Gustav," said Bent quietly, "you know I'm not one to tell tales. I'm not going to mention it to the police. I just want to know."

"I didn't kill Stig!"

"Course not, sonny. I just need to know why you were arguing with him."

Gustav thought it over for a moment. "Can you keep a secret, Bent? Promise you won't tell my Mum?"

Bent looked up at him. "Course not, you big daftie. I swear to death. *Ama'r halshug!*"

"Okay, then." Gustav paused. "A cigarette."

"What?" said Bent, confused. "You know I've given them up, Gustav. Plays havoc with my lungs."

"No, Bent. Me and a cigarette. Stig saw me smoking."

"I thought your Mum promised you a moped on your 18th if you didn't smoke?"

"That's the bloody problem, isn't it? Stig was furious when he caught me that night in the car park. Said how Mum and Karin would be so disappointed."

"Was he going to tell them?"

Gustav sat down on the wall, "Nah. Not Stig. He was a good guy. Just wanted to frighten me, I suppose. And he did put the wind up me. God, I was fuming. I told him to mind his own business. Wish I hadn't now…"

"And what happened then?"

"I quit, Bent. No more cigarettes for me."

"No, I mean that night."

"Oh," thought Gustav, "nothing. I cooled down when I got into the kitchen. Washing dishes is a mind-numbing job, it gave me plenty of time to think. To be honest, Bent, it was a relief to get the cigarette thing out in the open. I'd been dreading someone finding out. Not just Mum but Ida, too."

"And you didn't fight again with Stig?"

"No. It was all good. We even joked a bit together before he left with Mads. You can ask Ida."

"How is Ida, by the way?"

Gustav reddened and smiled. "Bloody wonderful?"

"Ha ha, sonny – you've got it bad! Have you asked her out yet, your…*chérie bon bon?*"

Gustav laughed. "Good one, Bent! I'm working myself up to it. Perhaps the Moonlight Bathe. If she's able to get away from that bloody Brix family for one night."

"Good idea, very romantic. So about Stig, that's it? Nothing else?"

"That's it, Bent," said Gustav, "God's honest truth." He pulled his finger across his neck, "*Ama'r halshug!*"

Bent grinned, pulled out a pack of cigarettes from his inner pocket and offered one to Gustav. "Here, son, these are my last two. After this, we both stop. Right?"

Gustav looked around the empty car park, then took one and smiled. "Cheers, Bent, you're the man!"

## CHAPTER 47

Lea tried Bent's number again. Why wasn't he answering? Where on earth was he? She was starting to worry. First the business with Stig and now Bent had disappeared. Hadn't she told him to take care? Just as she put her phone down on the sofa, the doorbell rang and she ran to answer it. About bloody time too.

"Hi Lea—"

"Mads? What on earth are you doing here? Look, I'm kind of busy right now—" She tried to shut the door, but he put his arm up.

"Please, Lea. Can I just explain?"

"Mads, there's no need to explain to me. We were finished a long time ago—"

He kept his hand on the door. "Please, Lea. It'll only take a couple of minutes—"

Lea groaned. "Oh, alright, come in then. But make it quick will you?" She was in two minds. On the one hand, she was worried about Bent and wanted to go looking for him. On the other hand, she was relishing the thought of getting an apology from Mads. Despite how much she insisted outwardly that she didn't want one.

Mads moved through to the living room and glanced fleetingly at the stereo, where a CD case was lying open on top of the player.

"Do you want it back?"

"What?"

"The Tue West CD. It's yours."

Mads sat down on one side of the sofa. "No, you keep it. I'm glad you like it."

There was plenty of room for the two of them, but Lea moved a pile of magazines from the armchair and sat there instead, waiting for him to start.

Mads smiled and pointed at the empty wine glass on the table. "Not going to offer me a drink?"

Lea started to stand up.

"Okay, okay, calm down!" He shifted slightly on the sofa and took a deep breath. "It's like this. Pernille and I broke up months ago."

She already knew that. Get to the point, Mads. Lea continued to sit in silence.

"I did love her. At least for a while. But, well, as you probably heard, she got bored of me and…" Mads hesitated.

Do not feel sorry for him, Lea. Bite your tongue and let him suffer. Lea didn't bat an eyelid. "And what, Mads?"

"Well, she cheated on me. Not just once. Several times…"

Well, wasn't that a surprise. Lea kept eye contact with Mads, but said nothing.

"That's when I decided to move back to Strandvig. The whole mess with Pernille and me, that was tough and embarrassing. But it was even more difficult to admit to myself that, as much as I wanted to, I just didn't fit in in Copenhagen. I missed life here, you know. Boring village life."

Lea was enjoying being the Queen of Cool. She simply sat and listened.

"You're not making this easy for me."

No. She wasn't, was she.

"And then I bumped into you at the Kro that night…"

Oh, here we go, this was going to be interesting… Lea didn't bat an eyelid, but just said, "Uh huh."

"You know I've always had feelings for you. And that night… I may be wrong here, but I thought you felt it too?"

141

Lea felt the hairs on the back of her neck rise. "Oh, really? So that's why you invited me to your place for a drink. And then ran off into the night, as soon as your precious Pernille called?"

"Lea, she called to tell me she was pregnant."

Lea felt hot. And sick to the bottom of her stomach.

Mads stood up. "She said she was pregnant and that the baby was mine. She was in a right state. Lea, I had to go to her. Believe me, if I had thought for a minute that you might come by…"

"Well, good for you for being Pernille's knight in shining armour. So it's all back on then between you, is it?" Lea tried not to sound aggressive, but this wasn't exactly the apology she had been expecting. She was angry at Mads. And Pernille too. Why on earth had she let Mads over the doorstep?

Mads looked wounded. "That's what I'm trying to explain! If you'll just let me finish…" He sat down on the sofa again. "When I went round there that night, I realised immediately that she wasn't giving me the full story."

A leopard never changes her spots, Lea. Or his, for that matter. She said simply, "Go on."

"I couldn't believe it – I didn't want to believe it. After all the lies I had heard from her in the past…."

Lea's shoulders dropped. "So she isn't pregnant then?"

Mads looked up. "Yes, I'm afraid she is."

Lea felt sick, again. Why did she let him do this to her? It was like being on a rollercoaster.

"What Pernille conveniently failed to mention is that she'd been seeing some other bloke since I moved out. She cheated on him. And then he moved out too—"

"What a right little charmer she is!" The bitch. Lea had known it all along.

"And then she found out she was pregnant. And called me."

"So the baby is yours then?"

142

"That's the thing. A couple of days later after Stig was found, when I got my head clear, I started asking her questions. Because the dates and times just didn't add up. There's no way I can be the father – it just didn't make sense. I was well off the scene by then."

"So why did she call you?"

"She panicked. She knew all along it was the other bloke's baby. But he had scarpered and she thought I would be a soft touch."

Lea glowered. Yes, of course, she did.

He looked into her eyes. "Thank God I didn't fall for it. I really wanted to make a fresh start here in Strandvig."

"Well, yes, that must be a great relief." Lea tried to sound neutral, but was fuming inside. So this is why he wanted to explain? To make himself feel better?

"Thanks for letting me explain. I'm so sorry about that night, Lea. Really."

He leaned over and reached out to take her hands. "Now, if you can find your way to forgive me, Lea, I'd really like us to—"

Lea's telephone rang.

## CHAPTER 48

Gustav slammed the door behind him and started running down the three flights of stairs, pushing the earbuds into his ears. He fished inside his inside right pocket for his bike key. True to form, it wasn't there. Shit! He knelt down on the landing, his Fjällräven rucksack making a large thump as it hit the linoleum.

Gustav pulled open the flap and plunged in a hand, rooting around the bottom of the bag. And pulled out a tightly wound wad of bank notes, secured with a beige plastic band.

The tick-tick-tick of the stair light stopped and he sat back against the wall, winded. He would call Ida.

CHAPTER 49

*B*ʑʑʑʑʑʑʑʑʑ. *B*ʑʑʑʑʑʑʑʑʑ. *B*ʑʑʑʑʑʑʑʑʑ.
The muffled vibrating outside stopped. Bent sat down on a large can of paint. His arms were sore from banging on the door and he had given up shouting five minutes ago. He pulled on the door handle and shook it. Ha! There he was, rattling on the bars! Holy Helle would have a field day when she found out. And when she did find out, she would probably want to shut him back in again! Ha!

He fished in his shopping bag and dug out his trusty thermos. Luckily for him there was still a drop of strong black coffee in it. And still warm to boot. He swallowed the coffee and took off his yellow beanie. He couldn't think properly with a hat on. Thinking caps? Who on earth came up with that nonsense?

*B*ʑʑʑʑʑʑʑʑʑ. *B*ʑʑʑʑʑʑʑʑʑ. *B*ʑʑʑʑʑʑʑʑʑ.
He was in a right pickle. Stuck inside the storage hut. With his box of tools – and his vibrating telephone – outside. Not exactly his best moment. But how was he to know that there would come a mighty great gust of wind and slam the door, just as he was inside fetching an old towel to kneel on while he worked? He would just have to wait it out.

It was actually rather cosy in there, with the noise of the wind howling outside. He started to rummage around the shelves at the very back of the hut. Maybe he might get lucky and find another bottle of *Gammel Dansk* lurking there in the cobwebs.

He stood on his tiptoes, peered upwards and started working downwards. Danish flags, towels, painters' overalls. Paintbrushes that had seen better days, jars of screws and lengths of rope. Algae remover, linseed oil, white spirit. Bottles, bottles everywhere, but sadly not a drop of *Gammel Dansk* to drink.

Well, well, well. What did we have here? Bent's mind went into overdrive. He forgot for a moment that his arms were still aching from hammering on the door of the storage hut and reached out as far as he could. But aching or no, his Lilliputian arm wasn't long enough to reach the back corner of the bottom shelf. The folding trestle table was leaning against the shelves, blocking his way. There was nothing for it, he would need to move it out of the way. The table smelt damp and was covered in scratches. But covered with a tablecloth it became the high table for all the social events at the Vikings. Like next week's Moonlight Bathe…

Bent pushed the trestle table to the side and triumphantly claimed his prize from the bottom shelf. A pot of luminous paint… He shook it up and down. Yes, it was full. It had never been opened. Just the ticket! Holy Helle would have kittens! He chuckled to himself and thought that, yes, Lea was right, he was just a big kid.

*Bzzzzzzzzzzz. Bzzzzzzzzzzz. Bzzzzzzzzzzz.*

It was probably Lea again. He knew he should have called her after he left Elvira's place. Elvira had even nagged him about it, but he had wanted to fix the door first. He didn't want that incident with Ellen stuck in the hut on his conscience one minute longer. So now he had both Ellen and Lea on his conscience. Oh well, if he waited long enough, surely they would come and find him. He'd sit tight and enjoy the last of his coffee in peace. He started to reminisce about the early days of the Vikings. Hard to believe that the storage hut had been their communal changing hut in those days. Ach, and all that had changed now. Separate changing huts, bah!

Thirty years ago he had opened the door of the hut to find that the local kids had sneaked in late at night and been using the place as their secret den. Leaving behind them a well-thumbed copy of a girlie mag, a few empty bottles of *Tuborg* on the shelves and the lingering smell of stale cigarettes. He felt in his pocket. He could really do with one right now, but he had given his word to Gustav.

That's when it hit him. He suddenly felt very weak and had to steady himself on the door. He had to speak to Daniel. But how on earth was he going to get out?

CHAPTER 50

Lea stared down at her phone. Mads drew back in his seat, suddenly on the offensive.

"Aren't you going to answer it?"

The phone continued to ring.

"Or is it Daniel?"

"Daniel? Why would it be Daniel?"

She looked down at the screen again. It was Daniel. No doubt about it. How on earth did Mads know that? What the hell was going on?

"Come off it, Lea. I've seen the way he looks at you. Everyone has."

"You're making it up—"

"Johnny was just mentioning it last night."

Lea tried to pry her eyes away from her phone.

"Oh, he was, was he?" Why was Johnny always poking his nose into other people's business? She put her phone down on the table beside her, trying not to blush. Daniel was trying to call her? So she hadn't imagined it. Wow. Maybe this Old Maid could still turn heads? Lea stood up.

"And even if it was, Mads Sørensen? What on earth would that have to do with you? That's absolutely none of your bloody business! Who do you think you are? You come back to Strandvig and think you can just waltz back in to our lives—"

Mads put his hands up in defence. "Okay, okay, I'm sorry!" He thought for a second and leaned in towards her. "Maybe I'm a little jealous? I just hoped that you and I might be able to—"

Lea moved towards the door. "Enough of that crap, Mads! Things have changed around here. Me included. And for your information, Mads Sørensen, I'm actually waiting for Bent to call!"

She stood up. "I think it's best you leave now…"

## CHAPTER 51

Lea closed the door of her flat, took a deep breath and sat down. She looked at her phone one more time, just to be sure. Daniel had tried to call. Something that both thrilled and terrified her. What on earth did he want? More to the point – her heart rate beginning to break into a slow jog – what on earth did she want? Her mind, meanwhile, was already in full sprint and racing backwards, then forwards, in a hundred different directions. Maybe she (and Mads, Johnny and the rest of Strandvig) was reading Daniel all wrong and it was part and parcel of the police enquiries about Stig. Maybe he had dialled the wrong number – it happened (usually to Bent). But why hadn't Daniel left a message? Damn! She was too scared to call him back.

She willed the telephone to ring again. Damn that Mads was right. And damn that Mads was sitting there with her when the phone rang. He was never where you expected him to be and was always in the wrong place at the wrong time!

Five minutes later there was still only deafening silence from her phone. There was no point in sitting here waiting for Daniel to call, she had better go look for Bent. And why hadn't Bent returned her calls? Men. She threw her telephone into her bag – checking one more time that the volume was set to the maximum – pulled on her winter boots, wrapped her grey scarf around her neck and decided she would bike up to Strandhøj Kro. Perhaps Bent had stopped off there for a half pint and had got a little too cosy sitting up on his little perch of a bar stool? Though, to be fair to him, he was more likely being held hostage by Karsten and his never-ending supply of witticisms. It was worth a shot.

Lea turned in to the hotel car park and was somewhat disappointed to find Johnny, the eyes and ears of Strandvig, wheeling a barrel towards the cellar steps. She kept her head down and wheeled her bike over to the stand, hoping he wouldn't hear the sound of the tyres on the ice.

"Hey there, beautiful!"

She pretended not to hear and bent over to lock her bike. If he dared make one remark about Mads, she would tear his stupid head off.

"Hey, Lea!" Johnny was grinning like a Cheshire cat and made a big play of looking at his watch. "We don't normally see you here this time of day. Sorry, beautiful, but if you want some lunch you're out of luck. We closed a quarter of an hour ago."

Lea shrugged. Steady now, Lea! You're a big girl, no cupcakes this year. Don't let him get the better of you. "That's okay. I don't want lunch."

Johnny stopped wheeling the barrel and leant his arms on the trolley. "Oh, I get you. New diet is it? Karsten's on a diet. A sea—"

Lea had heard this one a thousand times before. She would not fall into the trap. No, she would not. She puffed up her chest and mimicked Johnny's voice. "A seafood diet, Johnny? 'He sees food and eats it?'"

Johnny didn't seem in the least put out by her rather impressive, she thought, imitation of him.

"Okay, not seafood then. Maybe you're on a whisky diet, like me?"

"Whisky?"

"Yeah, beautiful. I'm on a whisky diet…and I've already lost three days!"

Lea groaned inwardly. She had fallen into the trap. Again. "For the love of God, Johnny, it's already bad enough with Karsten without you starting… Look, I need to find Bent, is he inside?" She almost spat the words out, surprising herself. Good for you, Lea.

151

"Bent? Dunno, beautiful. He wasn't in earlier, but I couldn't swear to it. I've been out here for the last five or ten minutes."

"Okay, thanks." She threw her bike key into her bag and headed towards Strandhøj's main entrance.

"Hey, are you alright?"

Lea turned around. Do not feed the troll. Do not feed the troll. "Yes, Johnny. Perfectly, fine." She continued walking, well aware that Johnny's eyes were still fixed upon her.

"You look a bit…what's the word? Agitated? Your face is all red."

Lea swirled around. Johnny took out a Prince, looking the picture of innocence. Thanks a million, Johnny, that's just what a girl wants to hear. Lea unravelled her woollen scarf in an attempt to get some cool air on her face. "So would you, Johnny, if you had just cycled here as fast as I did. Not that anyone would ever accuse you of getting much exercise…" Ugh, do not provoke him, Lea, that's just what he wants.

He lit up the cigarette and took a deep drag, choosing his words very carefully. "Nah, I'm not like you, Lea. I don't go chasing men on my bike. First Mads at the Kayak Club and now Bent here at the Kro? Make your mind up, woman. Who's next in line? Young Gustav? Or, hey, there's always me… How about it, beautiful?"

Lea felt like she had been physically slapped in the face. The parts of Lea's face that weren't already red changed to crimson. She fleetingly considered making a biting remark about Johnny and Karin but, being the nice girl she was, the thought stayed right there inside her head. She simply kept walking towards the Kro and opened the main door, trying to hold her head as high as possible.

Lea stamped her boots on the mat and smoothed down her hair the best she could. She caught her reflection in the reception mirror and was dismayed to find that Johnny was right: her face was the colour of a beetroot. No sight or sound of Bent or anyone else, Lea headed into the bar, pulled towards the sound of lounge music. Candles still burned at the tables and there was a comforting aroma of bacon about the place, but the Kro was now essentially empty after the short, sharp lunchtime rush. A couple of businessmen in dark suits sat by the bay window with empty plates in front of them, finishing their drinks. She could see from the small frying pan on the table that one of them had ploughed through today's dish of the day, *æggekage med flæsk*. Freshly-cooked omelette topped with strips of crispy bacon, slices of fresh tomato and finely chopped chives. Lea's stomach rumbled – she had completely missed lunch due to Mads' appearance and Bent's disappearance. She was just about to leave when there was a noise from behind the bar and a small head popped up.

"Hi, poppet! You gave me a right fright, you did. I was just cleaning out the bottles back here. In for a late lunch are you? The kitchen's closed, but I'm sure we can fix you up with something nice. What can we get you—"

"Thanks, Lisbeth, that's really kind, but I'm not here for lunch. I'm actually just in looking for Bent. He was supposed to call me earlier and now I can't get through to him. You haven't seen him by any chance, have you?"

"No, poppet. He hasn't been in here today. But nothing unusual in that, he normally comes in later in the day. Want me to give him a message?"

"No, I'm sure he'll be in touch. Probably got tied up somewhere. No big deal."

Lisbeth was immediately on high alert. "Not like you to be out looking for him. Is something up, poppet?"

Lea tried her best to diffuse the situation. If she was worried, Lisbeth would break into a full scale panic. "I'm sure he's fine. Really. It's just me overreacting after what happened to... Well, you know."

Lisbeth clutched a bottle of *Gammel Dansk* to her chest. "Oh my God, yes. I hope he hasn't gone missing too. I just couldn't bear it!"

"Who's gone missing, my love?" Karsten returned, carrying a fresh supply of white damask table cloths.

"Bent!"

"Bent's gone missing?" Karsten put down the cloths and hitched up his trousers. "Is this true, Lea?"

"It's probably nothing. Honestly, Karsten, it was silly of me to come out. He's probably just delayed. You know what he's like when he's with one of his ladies."

"The old devil, yes! Lisbeth, my love, don't worry that pretty little head of yours, we'll get to the bottom of this. Just tell us who Bent's hooked up with at the moment? Is it Gerda or Elvira?" He winked at Lea. "Or maybe it's both!"

Lisbeth put the *Gammel Dansk* down on the bar and steadied her trembling hands on it. "E-E-E-Elvira, I think."

Karsten put a protective arm around her. "There, there, my love. You see, we're making progress already. Have you got her phone number? Great, probably best if I give her a call. You just sit down here." He took the phone from Lisbeth's shaking hand.

Lea remembered her own phone and fished it out of her pocket. Still nothing. She wasn't sure what was more infuriating or worrying, the lack of contact from Bent, or Daniel.

Karsten nodded and paced the floor. "...two hours ago? Thanks, Elvira. Yes, I know, but you can't tell him can you? A stubborn old goat. Once he gets hold of something, he hangs on for dear life and won't let go. Ha ha – that's what she said last night! Let me just check." He signalled to Lisbeth that he wanted a pen. "Yes, 4 pm next week should be fine. How many? Righty-ho. I'll put down twelve – I know what an appetite you and your girls have. Ha ha, yes! I'm sure that's what Bent said last night! Okay, thanks – *ciao!*"

Lisbeth looked at Lea, who rolled her eyes. Karsten switched off the phone and gave Lisbeth a hug.

"I'm better than Barnaby – mystery solved!"

"So he is alive then? He's with Elvira?" Lisbeth still looked panic stricken.

"He was with Elvira last night, he left her this morning—"

"But where is he now?" Lisbeth wasn't comforted at all.

"Let me finish, my love! Elvira said he left there about two hours ago. Said he was heading for the Vikings, to fix the door of the storage hut. You know, where Ellen got stuck that time."

"But why didn't he call me? He promised to come round first thing this morning." Lea, while relieved that Karsten had managed to locate the oldest swinger in town, felt rather foolish having set the whole of Strandvig upside down looking for him.

"Elvira told him he should call you before you left. But you know what he's like, Lea. Said he was in a hurry."

"But if that was two hours ago, surely he should be finished by now? Why doesn't he answer his bloody phone?"

"Perhaps the oldest swinger in town is off on another, ahem, job? Shall I try phoning Gerda?"

"No, thanks, Karsten. I'll try the Vikings." She wrapped her scarf around her neck and pulled on her gloves. "Just wait until I get my hands on him."

Lisbeth looked worried. "You won't hurt him, will you, poppet?"

CHAPTER 52

There was no-one at the Vikings today. The sea had frozen over and Helle, backed by the Committee, had officially closed the club for the next five days. Or until the Danish weather Gods looked down with mercy at the bathers and allowed a partial thaw – just enough to be able to cut a decent sized hole in the ice. The Vikings were disappointed that they wouldn't have their daily dose of icy seawater, but respected the laws of nature. Patience was most certainly a virtue.

For a moment Lea was disappointed, thinking that the bird had flown the premises. But the main gate was unlocked, and she could see bike tracks and footprints on the other side. Her phone still showed nothing. Not a peep from Bent. Or, even worse, from Daniel – the suspense was killing her. She let herself in, pulling her bike with her.

She was looking forward to her confrontation with Bent. Just like the wife in Tam O' Shanter, Lea had been 'nursing her wrath to keep it warm' during the hour she had been trying to track him down. Not that she planned to use any physical force. Lisbeth, upset at Bent's disappearance, but also concerned by what Lea might do to him – if and when she located him – had needed a good few minutes of soothing talk from Karsten and Johnny before she had allowed Lea to leave their premises. No, Lea had repeatedly assured her, she only wanted to give Bent a good telling off. *À la* Holy Helle.

Lea leant her bike against the fence and carefully made her way across the icy boards. She tried the doors of the bathing huts and the sauna. Everything was locked down, as was to be expected, but nonetheless it felt uncannily quiet. And yet, if the club had been open for business, with bathers turning up within the next few minutes, she would have revelled in the silence and the chance to have the place all to herself. She shivered and pulled her scarf up further around her ears, anything to keep the wind out, and continued round the back towards the storage hut. There – lo and behold – was Bent's bike. And the club toolbox. But where on earth was the man himself? The jetty was deserted.

"Bent! Bent!" She felt silly calling out with only the seagulls to hear her. *C-l-a-n-g!* The noise of the main gate banging. Lea jumped out of her skin and turned to look but no-one was there. She hadn't bothered to lock the gate behind her and it must have blown open. She was getting sick and tired of this. "Bent?!"

"Hallo?" A muffled voice and came from inside the hut.

"Bent? It's Lea!"

"What? Hallo?" A noise of shuffling footsteps.

"Are you in there?" Lea rattled on the door handle, but to no avail. "It's me – Lea!"

"Pull, Lea Mus! For God's sake!"

"Okay, okay, keep your hair on!" This is the thanks she got? She pulled hard but the door wouldn't budge. She put her head right next to the door and shouted.

"It's stuck! Which is lucky for you, Bent Bang, because I've got a bone to pick with you."

"I know the door's stuck, Lea Mus."

"Then why on earth didn't you call me? I've been all over Strandvig."

"My phone's outside. In the toolbox."

Lea looked down and started to laugh. "Oh, Bent, wait until Holy Helle hears about this!"

Bent banged the door. "Lea, I want you to phone Daniel! Quickly!"

Lea leaned against the door, immensely enjoying that Bent was in a pickle. And she had no intention of phoning Daniel, whatever the emergency. "Oh calm down, would you. I hardly think we need to call in the Strandvig police force for this one. Let me call Johnny or Mads to come and—"

Bent's voice went up a scale. "No, not Johnny!"

Lea leaned forward. "Okay, okay, keep your beanie on. I'll call Mads—"

Bent now went into falsetto. "Not Mads. DANIEL. Do it NOW. I know who killed Stig!"

Okay, now Bent was losing it. "Bent, have you been drinking?"

"No, Lea Mus. *Ama'r halshug!* Listen to me. I could smell smoke when I went into the storage hut the morning we found Stig."

"Uh huh?" Lea was wondering whether she shouldn't be calling an ambulance. Perhaps it was hypothermia? After all, the daft old bird had probably been in there for over an hour.

"I recognised the smell, Lea Mus."

Lea looked behind her at the toolbox, briefly considering trying to break Bent out herself. But maybe he needed medical assistance? It would be good to have back up. She fished her phone out of her bag and took off her gloves. Daniel or Mads. Hmm – which one? "Bent, what are you on about?"

Bent's voice was calmer now. "The only person who had been in here that week was Ellen, and she doesn't smoke."

"Obviously." Lea decided to call Mads. He would be back at the Kayak Club by now and would know what to do. And he was Bent's friend after all. Mads would probably see her call and think that she had changed her mind, all ready to run right back to him and his 'chilled white wine'. That would serve him right.

"Lea, we know the killer was in here. He used the hammer from the toolbox. Probably drank the bottle of *Gammel Dansk* too."

"The killer smokes and drinks? Bent, honestly. You've just described most of Strandvig—" Lea decided she would call Mads. Daniel would think Bent was completely off his rocker.

158

"Mads and Johnny used to come here to the hut when they were just lads. Call Daniel! NOW! Do you hear me, Lea Mus?!"

"Hi beautiful, need some help?" Lea almost cricked her neck, so fast it spun round, to find Johnny standing behind her, large as life. He was grinning from ear to ear and holding up a monkey wrench from the tool box.

Lea immediately forgave Johnny for being such an idiot back at the Kro – help was help, wherever it came from. "Oh my God, Johnny – you gave me such a fright. Where on earth did you come from?"

"I followed you down here from the Kro. Lisbeth was worried you might do Bent some harm. You know me, always keen to lend a hand! Even if it is bloody cold." He shivered and lit up a Prince.

"Oh, thank God, Johnny. Bent's stuck inside – must have been here for hours and he's started talking nonsense. Can you help me to get this door open? I'm really worried that—"

"Lea? Lea? Call Daniel, call DANIEL!" Bent was battering on the door for all his worth.

"Sure, beautiful. Have you tried pulling the handle?"

Lea shot him a look.

"Just kidding! I'll have to force it open. But it won't be pretty and there'll be some damage—"

"I don't care. Let's get him out!"

Johnny raked around in the toolbox. "Your call, beautiful. But make sure you tell Holy Helle it wasn't my fault!"

Lea didn't give a fig – or a cupcake – as to what Holy Helle might think. Right this minute she was considering calling Lisbeth, who would certainly rally round for Bent with some brandy and a bowl of steaming hot soup.

"Lea? Is that Daniel with you?" Bent's voice was feeble again.

"See what I mean, Johnny? Now he's hearing things. Make it quick, will you!"

Johnny stubbed out his cigarette and pulled out a crowbar. "Oh boy, that's a long one... Ha ha – that's what she said last night!"

Lea wasn't in the mood for jokes. She put her hand on the door and shouted as loud as she could. "Move your hands away from the door, Bent! We're coming in!"

The third time that Johnny jimmied the door worked a charm. "Open sesame!" Johnny opened the door and Bent fell forward, almost knocking Lea over.

"Oh, Bent, you poor thing! Let's get you over to the Kro and get you warmed up!"

Bent leant on her arm and tried to adjust his eyes to the light.

"Johnny, is that you? You bastard!"

"Hey, I just helped to get you out of there, old man! I'm sorry about the door but Lea thought—"

Bent looked up imploringly at Lea. "Lea Mus, listen to me! You have to call Daniel. Now! It was Johnny – he was the one who killed Stig!"

Lea tried to take Bent's arm. "Calm down, Bent, you're not thinking straight. Let's get you over to the Kro—"

Bent's strength re-emerged, accompanied by a flaring red colour in his cheeks. He shook his fist at Johnny, eyes glaring. "Don't you dare come near me! I know it was you! Lea Mus, get Daniel!"

Johnny threw the crowbar in the toolbox and rolled his eyes. "I see what you mean, Lea. The old guy's off his rocker. Hypothermia? I'll call an ambulance—"

Bent wasn't going to be fobbed off so easily. "It was you who had been in the hut the morning Stig was found. I could smell it. I would recognise that smell anywhere. It smelt of you, your cigarettes. That's what was so odd that morning when I opened the door. I only realised it just now."

"So I smoke! So do you. And Gustav. Yeah, I saw you both in the car park last night, Bent. Doesn't mean anything."

"You came here when you were a kid, didn't you, Johnny? You and Stig and your schoolmates. It was the same smell as back then. I would bet my life on it. *Ama'r halshug!*"

"You're barking up the wrong tree, Bent. Besides, who's going to believe the ramblings of an old man?"

"Why? Why did you do it, Johnny?"

Lea looked on in disbelief. Bent certainly didn't look the worse for wear after his enforced confinement. On the contrary, now that the colour had returned to his cheeks, she'd never seen him more alive. But the quantum leap to Johnny having murdered his colleague, his friend? And yet... Bent had planted a tiny seed of doubt, and she forced herself to see where it might lead.

She took Bent's arm and looked him in the eye. "Bent, we'll get this sorted out."

She picked up her bag and turned around. "Johnny, I'm sorry but I'm going to have to ask. Just one question. How did you know that I went to the Kayak Club the night Stig was killed?"

"Lea, not you too? Bent is off his rocker and now you're not making sense." He lit up a cigarette. "Let's get out of here."

Events were slowly beginning to bump into each other, then link up in Lea's mind. "No-one knew I had gone to see Mads at the Kayak Club that night."

"So?" Johnny looked out to sea. "What's that got to do with me?"

"I didn't tell anyone. Not even Bent."

Silence.

"And yet you knew. You mentioned it several times. That you had seen me chasing after Mads..."

"What if I did? I was jesting, Lea. You know me, that's how I am."

"Johnny, you mentioned that I was at the Kayak Club. And you couldn't possibly have known that unless you yourself had been out that night."

161

"Right couple of detectives we have here. And I came to help you out! Why do I bother? I'm leaving."

Bent grabbed Johnny's arm. "Why did you do it? For God's sake, man, Stig was your friend!"

"Get out of my way!" Johnny pushed Bent hard and knocked him down onto his knees on the ice.

Lea stood in his path. Bent had started an avalanche in her mind and she decided to take a leap. "And what about that anonymous phone call to the police, the day after Mads and Karin had a drink together. Was that you, trying to get your own back? I think you owe us an explana—"

"I don't owe you anything." He picked up the monkey wrench from the toolbox and headed straight for her. "Now get out of my way before I smash that beautiful face of yours!"

Heavy footsteps pounded on the boards and two large figures appeared around the corner. It was the Sheriff and the Lone Ranger.

162

# CHAPTER 53

Two police officers, the last men on the scene, were handcuffing Johnny and reading him his rights. Mads had his arm around Bent, who was covered from head to toe in blankets and once more sitting on the bench inside the storage hut.

"But how did you know we were here?"

Daniel smiled at her. "You called your friend, Mads?"

Lea shook her head. "He's not my friend—" Now she was blushing. "Well, you see Bent wanted me to call someone and—"

"You must have pressed a key by mistake. Mads answered your call, but you didn't speak. He was just about to hang up when he heard the voices in the background – you and Johnny shouting."

"And Mads called the police?"

"No, he was up at the Kro when you called. It was sheer co-incidence that he saw us there. We were there to pick up Johnny, but he had flown the coop." Daniel nodded over to the suspect. "Johnny's going to be, how shall I say it, helping us with our enquiries."

"So you do think it was Johnny? Oh my God. I mean, I know Bent is adamant – something about the smell of cigarettes in the hut that morning. And Johnny had somehow seen me that night at the Kay—" Lea stopped. Perhaps this wasn't something she really should be sharing with Daniel.

"All in good time, Lea. You've had a bit of a shock." He touched her arm gently. "We've got some pretty strong forensic evidence. So I'm pretty sure we've got our man."

"Oh, right. Thank God for that. Um, does that mean I can go now?"

"Sure. I need to speak to Bent immediately, but you go on home and get warmed up. We can get your statement later."

Daniel slowly walked her up to the main gate and held it open for her, smiling. "By the way, Lea. I've been trying to ring you. Why didn't you call me back?"

## CHAPTER 54

Bent and Mads were still sitting on the bench in the storage hut, drinking cups of hot sweet tea from a thermos, supplied by Lisbeth, while Johnny was being questioned by the officers. As they were all packing up to leave, Bent stood up and growled. "Coward! How could you kill a friend?!"

Johnny didn't move but stood calmly against the railing. "Friend? Stig was never my friend. Mr Goody Two Shoes had no ambition. Look at what happened with him and Karin. He had her and then he let her go."

"You killed him to get Karin?"

Johnny smirked. "Oh, but I didn't kill him, Bent. You see, it was all just a silly accident."

"Accident? Accident, *min røv!*"

"Now, now, Bent – mind your language! We came down here and sneaked over the fence. Just like old times, when we were lads. You even said it yourself, didn't you? Found the bottle of *Gammel Dansk* in the shed and we sat there, getting drunk together. And then Stig... He must have had a bit too much and fell in the water—"

"Liar! Stig never touched spirits. He was a beer man, ask Karsten!"

"Well that's his word against mine, isn't it? And he's not here to say otherwise."

Now Mads was on his feet. "And you didn't help him?"

"Like I said, I was drunk. Fell asleep in the storage hut and, when I woke up, he was gone. So you see, it was all just an accident... I'm sure the judge will agree with me."

"Then why didn't you say anything before? You've been quiet all this time, with the police questioning anybody and everybody. And poor Karin – you've been hanging around her – you didn't think she deserved to know what happened? Why didn't you say? It doesn't make sense!"

Johnny inhaled and looked Bent straight in the eye. "Because you lot wouldn't have believed me anyway. Would you?"

"Okay, folks, it's time to go home now." Daniel gave the nod to the officers to take care of Bent.

Bent looked up at Daniel and pleaded. "Don't believe him, Daniel, he's lying!"

"Don't you worry, Bent. He can't talk his way out of technical evidence."

# CHAPTER 55

An air of silence had descended over Strandvig since Johnny's arrest. The speculation and rumours in the week following Stig's death had fired up the whole community, outraged that one of their own had been murdered, but there were a few who had secretly enjoyed the sudden notoriety and thrill of the chase. The fact that one of their own was now believed to be the culprit had changed the mood to darkness and sadness.

Kenneth continued to open the doors of *Brdr. Frandsen* every morning on the dot at 9.45am as usual, but felt no joy in making his small outdoor *tableaux*. Henrik tried to gee him up, even digging deep into his short pockets and ordering extra supplies for the shop from their pusher in the south of France. An English dealer who specialised in finding the most fantastic wrought iron pieces from rural farms and selling them on at vastly inflated prices (the farmers enjoying the money, as much as the idea that townies should want to display such old junk in their fine urban houses). But it was slow going and Henrik, too, was losing motivation.

Kenneth arranged the deerskins on the frosty bench outside the shop and was just lighting the candles in the large black lanterns on either side – accompanied by a very audible sigh – when he heard young excited voices behind him. It was Karin out with a crocodile of kids from *Æblegården*. Though the Danes are light-years behind the Brits when it comes to queuing, Danish nursery children are world experts in forming lines, and walking hand-in-hand, two by two.

Kenneth didn't need to look at the calendar to know what day it was. If the toddlers were out and about, it must be *tur dag* – Thursday.

"*Godmorgen*, Karin! Morning, children!" Kenneth looked further down the crocodile to see who was bringing up the rear. "*Godmorgen*, Jannick!"

"*Godmorgen*, Kenneth!" The kids were bundled up in their regulation ski suits, thermal gloves, thermal hats, thermal balaclavas, thermal boots and undoubtedly, under all the other layers, thermal underwear. Or at least woollen underwear. Reflective tags, in various shapes and sizes, hung like Christmas tree ornaments from their ski suits. Despite the sub-zero temperatures they were smiling from ear to ear.

"Where are you off to this morning, kids?"

"The station!" They chorused.

Karin wasn't taking them into town today, or planning to take them on the train at all. The station's close proximity to the nursery made it the number one stop on their morning walk. The children would line up, two by two, hand-in-hand, along the platform and wave for all they were worth when they saw the train arriving. The train stopped at Strandvig station, regardless of whether there were passengers getting on or off, but the children were of the firm belief that flagging down the train was absolutely essential. If they didn't wave, it wouldn't stop. The regular train driver knew this and, in turn, would roll down the window and give them a wave back.

"Are you going into Copenhagen?"

Karin was about to answer but was eclipsed by Mathias. What he lacked in years (though he was very proud to tell anyone who would listen that he was a whole three-and-a-half plus two-weeks-old) he made up in joyful spirit, always willing to make conversation with anyone who would listen. "*Nej*! We're going to the beach!"

Kenneth looked aghast. "In this weather?"

168

"You sound just like my dad. *Ja!* It's going to be so much fun!"

Kenneth didn't look convinced. And was having a very hard time putting on a smile this morning, even though the children's enthusiasm was normally highly contagious, even to the most pessimistic in the village. Word had it that the mouth of cranky old Bertil Bruun (the bike dealer who would just as happily hit you with a bicycle pump as sell you one) had turned 180 degrees one morning – no doubt accompanied by a lot of cranking and clanging – when the crocodile of children passed his bike shop. Bertil's wife, Anne, had called the Strandvig police, mistaking him for an intruder.

Kenneth whispered in Karin's ear. "Can they come in and get a hard-boiled sweetie?"

"No whispering! My Mum says you're not allowed to whisper!" Little Mathias was also vociferous on the rules of etiquette.

Kenneth mouthed silently to Karin. "High maintenance Maria's child?"

She nodded and winked.

"*Bolcher! Ja!*" The other kids, who either had better hearing or were less worried about Kenneth's *faux pas*, cheered in unison and charged towards the entrance.

Kenneth moved closed to Karin. "I have to leave the shop whenever Maria comes in, and leave Henrik to deal with her. My nerves can't stand it. She questions absolutely everything and expects special treatment. And not one positive word about anything or anyone. Not a single one. A vile woman."

Karin smiled. "She can be rather…demanding."

"No wonder the husband is out on the town every night. Henrik heard he was spotted in Copenhagen again last night. With not one, but two, young women draped all over him…"

"Quietly now, kids! And don't touch anything!" Jannick followed the line of kids, all of them stamping their snowy boots on the large black doormat as they entered.

169

Henrik, who was behind the counter, removing Lisa Nilsson from her box, looked up and shouted a hearty *Godmorgen* to the kids. He was immediately by Kenneth's side, complete with two large glass mason jars. Then, having had second thoughts, he bounced back to the counter, opened the drawer and removed two pairs of long sleek, silver, Danish design tongs. They wouldn't look out of place on a surgeon's table. And were equally, clinically, clean. Henrik was fond of the nursery kids, with their red-faced cherub cheeks. But rather less fond of their persistently dripping winter noses. The children were regular guests in the shop and, over time, Henrik had noted a worrying tendency when it came to runny noses. After a few seconds the children would rub the goo onto their sleeves, gloves or worse – Henrik shuddered – lick it off with their tongues. He was just pondering whether to fetch the hand sanitizer, but was cut short or, to be more precise, cut off, surrounded by a ring of eager children.

Henrik and Kenneth gave each jar a hearty shake to release the boiled sweets, unscrewed the lids and got ready to fish out the sweets with the tongs, ready to drop into the waiting sticky hands. Jannick instructed the kids to get back into line. Two rows. "*Kongen af Danmark* here on the left, strawberry here on the right!" Surprisingly the aniseed sweets were more popular than the strawberry ones. King Christian's physician had obviously been on to something.

Mathias – also defender of the shy – ushered his sister Mathilde into the right queue for the right flavour. And very gracefully asked Kenneth if his little sister might be allowed one extra strawberry sweet. "It's for Ninka Rabbit, you know."

Kenneth, his own mood lifting by the second, felt bad about little Mathias. It couldn't be easy growing up with Maria and Martin for parents. He also felt a little ashamed that he hadn't been as aware as he usually was of others.

He gave Mathias and Mathilde two extra sweets each, then touched Karin's arm lightly. "I'm so sorry we haven't been much help. Things just seem so – how can I put it – so dark right now. How are you doing?"

Karin picked out a strawberry sweet. "Oh, I'm surviving. Thank goodness I've got Sonja and Jannick helping me. When I'm at *Æblegården* with the kids I'm fine. There just isn't the time to think of anything else to be honest. But at home? Well, I just feel like I'm still in the middle of a nightmare. Without being able to wake up."

"Have you been out at all? Up at the Kro or—?" Kenneth immediately regretted his words. The last time he had seen Karin at the Kro had been the last night that he'd seen Johnny.

"No, not really. Not since they arrested Johnny. I just don't want to think about it at all, it's just too horrible. And these long, dark days don't help…"

"Are you coming to the Midnight Bathe?"

"Mads mentioned it—"

"You must come!" Henrik shouted over from the other side of the shop, where he was showing the kids the latest in safety candles. The kids were hanging on to his every word. And also keeping very keen toddler eyes on the mason jar and the tongs he was still holding in his hand.

"I have to say I don't really feel like it myself." Kenneth cocked his head to one side. "But I tell you what, if you go, I'll come too."

Karin laughed. "Is this a conspiracy? Because Mads has been really nagging me. Sonja too. I'm just not sure if I'm ready—"

Henrik turned the candles on and off using his remote control to more ooohs and aaahs. "But did Mads tell you what Bent said? Bent promised that he'd be putting on a show—"

"Uh oh? Bent?" Karin's eyes began to sparkle.

Kenneth clutched at his chest. "Bent? Oh my word – that man! What on earth can he be up to now? That sounds ominous!"

"That sounds fun!" Karin was intrigued. Maybe Mads was right and she needed a change of air. Cold, freezing, moonlight night air.

171

"Karin, Karin!" Asger, previously entranced by the safety candle display was now at her side and tugging furiously at her sleeve.

"Yes, what is it, *skat*?"

"I've pooped in my nappy!"

## CHAPTER 56

The moon shone down from a cloudless sky. The streets of Strandvig were deserted tonight, but there were rumblings coming from the Vikings where burning torches lit up the entrance. Holy Helle looked upwards and gave a silent, hurried thanks to the Dear Lord. The elements were behaving themselves and Helle was in her element. Commander Bro – egged on by Bent – had expressed interest in joining the Vikings, and Helle, with the full backing of the Committee, had invited him to be their guest of honour tonight. The Moonlight Bathe was one of the highlights of the winter season, ranking third place after the Christmas Eve Dip and the New Year Plunge, and the Vikings had turned out in force. As they always did, when lured by the prospect of free *smørrebrød* and hot coffee.

Ida, much to Gustav's astonishment (and Lisbeth's delight and Karsten's disbelief), had accepted Gustav's somewhat awkward invitation to be his date for the night. When he discovered the wad of money hidden in his rucksack that morning, he'd called Ida right away – the only person from the Kro he thought he could trust. He knew that, with the return of Stig's keys, everyone was a possible suspect. Ida had persuaded him to go straight to Strandvig police station and tell them everything he knew. Or didn't know. And was there waiting for him outside the police station when it was all over. Gustav had cracked and asked her out on the spot (and hadn't even been wearing his lucky underpants).

The young pair had been one of the first to arrive at the club and they were now wandering around the more remote parts of the bathing deck, hand in gloved hand.

"Maybe you should answer your telephone?" Gustav wasn't keen to let go of Ida's hand, but couldn't ignore the buzzing any longer.

Ida pulled it out. "It's Martin. Again."

"Martin the Peacock? Sorry – maybe I shouldn't call him that…"

Ida laughed. "Don't worry, everyone does. He's offered me a job as Office Junior in his firm."

"Oh." Like the rest of Strandvig, Gustav was well aware of Martin's reputation. Already irritated by Martin's seemingly constant need for contact with Ida, he was terrified by the scenario of Ida and Martin working together at even closer quarters. Without Mathias and Mathilde as chaperones. Gustav started to kick the boards with his foot. "Will you take it?"

"I've not decided yet. Looking after Mathias and Mathilde is a challenge, but fun. Working one on one with Martin would be… I don't know. And Maria doesn't seem too pleased about the idea. Pretty mad, actually. I could hear her screaming at Martin when I left last nig–" Ida looked up at Gustav. "Anyway, let's not talk about them, okay? Look – I'm switching off my phone."

Elvira and Gerda, doing their best to hide behind the sauna, watched the young pair and giggled.

"What's he waiting for, Gerda?"

"He does seem very shy. In our day, lads didn't hang around, did they? Oh – wait up – your granddaughter seems to be making a move!"

Ida had pulled Gustav's face down to hers and had given him a gentle kiss. They were both smiling and Gustav wrapped his arms around her. A million miles from the madding crowd, bathed in a grey halo of light.

Elvira sighed. "That's my girl! Okay, let's go and find Bent and get some food!"

Back on the main deck the party was in full swing. Robed and towel-clad figures were assembled together on the deck, huddled around braziers full of hot coals.

Ole and Bent had already pulled out the painter's trestle table from the back of the storage hut and set it up between the ladies and gents changing huts. Yrsa had brought her summery, strawberry print wax tablecloth from home and was smoothing it out and weighting it down at the corners with four large stones that her grandchildren had painted white. The Committee members and a few volunteers had each brought a large thermos of piping, hot coffee with them. Helle had texted them during the week, then phoned each of them late last night and again this afternoon to remind them of their civic duty. She hadn't physically spoken to them – they had learned by now not to answer when they saw her caller ID – so she had left messages with full instructions.

Helle herself brought three specially designated 'tea only' white coloured thermos' from the church hall. The unwitting volunteer who made the faux-pas of filling them with coffee at the Christmas Dip was now relegated to clean up duty.

Ellen's butcher shop supplied the *smørrebrød*. Always freshly made and always two types. Tonight there was *frikadeller med rødkål* – Ellen's homemade Danish meatballs, sliced up and topped with sweet, pickled red cabbage. And *franskbrød med ost* – French-style white baguette with slices of Danbo cheese, topped with rings of yellow and red pepper. Lined up side-by-side in huge, white, shallow cardboard butcher boxes. Normally Johnny would transport the *smørrebrød* down to the Vikings in the hotel minibus, but tonight Karsten and Lisbeth had made the run themselves, and been invited to stay on.

"Thank you so much for helping us out at the last moment, Mr Holm. Such a terrible business with Mr Rasmussen – God Rest His Soul! To think that Johnny Højer... Well, I really don't know what to say!"

Karsten looked down at his feet, "Yes, it's a bad business indeed. A shock to all of us. Not least my poor Lisbeth, here…" He put his arm around Lisbeth, who was dabbing her eyes with a hanky and looking very distraught – she wasn't comfortable standing on the bathing bridge. On the spot where it might have happened. "She always thinks the best of everyone, she does! But then again, she's from Aarhus you know!" Karsten winked at Helle, who merely stared back at him.

"Yes, Mr Holm. But I very much hope we can count on your support for our next event?" Helle was already thinking ahead to the logistics of the Easter Cleanse.

"Eh, yes. Yes, of course."

"So you'll be able to drive the *smørrebrød* for us?"

"Oh, yes, that won't be a problem. But it won't personally be me doing the driving – we'll be taking on a new man at the hotel."

"I very much hope you'll consider getting a background check done—"

"Oh, I really don't think that'll be necessary Mrs Brandt—"

"As recent events have shown us, Mr Holm, one can never be too sure!"

Karsten pointed over at two tall figures chatting beside the buffet table. "We've asked Mads if he's interested in the job. One of Strandvig's own. Now there's a man you can trust!"

Helle sniffed, straightened her back and ruffled her shoulders. "I very much hope so, Mr Holm. For all our sakes."

Lisbeth tried, and failed miserably, to hold back a very large sob. Karsten held her firmly and rubbed her back, as if he was burping a baby. "Come on, love – just let it all out!"

Helle searched for an area that wasn't totally engulfed by Karsten and put a firm hand on Lisbeth's coat sleeve. "There, there, Mrs Holm! Perhaps you might like to pop into the church tomorrow morning? I always feel a great sense of peace when sitting in the pew, communing with our maker."

Silence. It was impossible to tell if Lisbeth had physically stopped sobbing or was merely too deeply engulfed in Karsten's grasp for her sobs to be heard. A chorus of wolf whistles made the trio turn around.

The Moonlight bathers, clumped in little groups by the bathing steps, were all smiling, nodding and pointing in the same direction. A small stooped figure was slowly emerging from the gents changing hut. Complete with a bright yellow beanie on his head.

"Hey, there Bent! Why the bathing robe?"

"All that *Gammel Dansk* has finally gone to his head!"

"If it hadn't been for the yellow beanie, I wouldn't have recognised him!"

"Why so modest all of a sudden?"

"Not like you to hide your crown jewels, Bent!"

Bent sashayed over the boards – resplendent in a long dark velour bathing robe – in a quick step. Or was that the cha-cha-cha?

"Hey, that's not Bent. That's bloody Fred Astaire, that is!" quipped Karsten. Lisbeth managed to wriggle out of his grip and peered at the dancing figure in the moonlight.

Holy Helle winced. And not merely at Mr Holm's flagrant use of the 'b' word in her presence. She was beginning to get a bad feeling, a very bad feeling and moved closer for a better look at Bent. What on earth was that man up to now?

Bent, oblivious to the comments being fired his way, carried on his little dance towards the bathing steps, enjoying every moment. He stopped at the railings, did a small pirouette and – with a flourish – removed his beanie.

By now the crowd was chanting.

"Bent! Bent! Bent! Bent!"

He slowly untied the pleated cord of the robe, swung it round his head like a lasso three times, then let it fall to the ground. The group cheered. Helle cursed and prayed for divine intervention.

Bent turned towards the bathers. "Ladies and gentlemen, *Meine Damen und Herren, Mesdames et Messieurs!* For my next trick…"

He turned his back to them, slipped out of the robe and let it fall with a dramatic flourish. The crowd surged forward and spread out along the railings, watching as Bent descended into the water.

The crowd laughed, right on cue. Helle gasped for air. "Of all the..!"

Karsten let go of Lisbeth (who nearly collapsed due to the sudden unexpected release), slapped his thigh and let out a huge roar that carried all the way down the coast. "Moonlight Bathe? It's a moonlight bathe complete with a FULL MOON!"

Bent Bang's buttocks were coated with fluorescent paint.

CHAPTER 57

Bent slowly sipped his half pint and looked at the next one, already set up on the bar for him. Karsten was drying and polishing beer glasses. "That stunt you just pulled, Bent, is going to keep you supplied with these for a long time!" Once the last remnants of the *smørrebrød* and cake (with a noticeable lack of muffins from Lea) had been polished off at the Vikings, and the trestle table had been duly cleared, folded and put away at the very back of the storage hut under Helle's watchful eye, half of the bathers had moved on to Strandhøj in search – or so they claimed – of warming liquid refreshments. Par for the course, what they actually ordered on arriving at the Kro was, of course, something rather cold and very alcoholic.

"It certainly cheered me up no end, I can tell you!" Lisbeth, for once, also sitting down at the bar, cautiously sipped a small crystal glass, full to the brim with cherry wine. She didn't normally drink, but Karsten had administered it, saying that it would help to calm her down and build her up. "Medicinal purposes, love!" She very much doubted that *kirsebærvin* had healing properties. Then again, a lot of rosy-cheeked old biddies drank it, so really, who could say? Given that her toes still felt like two large blocks of ice, a whole two hours after Bent's antics on the bathing bridge, she wasn't going to argue. She raised her glass to Bent and looked him in the eye, "*Skål!*"

Lea, who was on a bar stool on the other side of Bent, joined in the toast and put her glass of white wine down in front of her and laughed. "I thought Holy Helle was going to read me the riot act for

179

not supplying cupcakes tonight. But you saved me, Bent Bang. Now it's you who's in hot water. Did you see Helle's face?"

Karsten continued polishing. "Course he didn't, Lea love. He was too busy pointing his luminous backside the other way!" He stopped, dishtowel in hand, and looked quizzical. "Now I come to think of it, Bent, how are you going to get that paint off? With some steel wool? Ouch!"

Bent nodded over at Elvira and Gerda, who were sitting with the rest of the Oldies at one of the long tables, each nursing a medicinal gin and tonic. There seemed to be copious amounts of medicine on tap tonight. Bent smiled contentedly. "No worries, Karsten, I've already had a few offers of help from some lovely ladies."

Lea looked at the two elderly ladies and rolled her eyes. She had learned not to be fooled by their demure exterior. "Oh my giddy aunt. Why does that not surprise me in the least?"

"Besides, where's the harm, Lea Mus? It was just my little bit of fun. I reckoned we all needed something to make us smile after the events of the past few days."

Lea popped a few peanuts into her mouth and rubbed the salt off her fingers. "Honestly, Bent, Helle looked like she wanted to crucify you."

Karsten looked up from pouring a pint. "Good job that toolbox of yours was locked away in the storage hut, then!"

Lisbeth clasped on to her *kirsebærvin* glass with both hands and hissed. "Really, Karsten?"

Bent's eyes turned sad for a moment. "Not that we're forgetting what happened to poor Stig, of course."

Lisbeth leaned over and put her arm around Bent. "No, Bent, of course we aren't."

Henrik and Kenneth had arrived at the Kro fifteen minutes earlier and were already in place, with a full bottle of Amarone and a plate of *petits fours* in front of them. Henrik managed to catch Bent's eye – Henrik's bulk wasn't easy to miss, especially as he was animatedly waving over, half-sitting, half-standing. He was very obviously the cat who had got the cream and was dying to tell someone, anyone the latest news. Lea and Bent succumbed and took their belongings over to join them.

"So did you hear about Johnny?" he said, grinning from ear to ear.

"Why, what's happened?" Lea wasn't really interested, she had heard nothing but rumours and gossip since the police had arrested him. All speculation, a lot of hearsay and most of it exaggerated and embroidered along the way. The Moonlight Bathe had been a welcome diversion.

"He finally confessed!"

"What? Who told you that?"

"A little birdy in the local constabulary told me!"

Kenneth looked over at Lea and winked. "I thought it was our Lea who had a direct line to them at the moment?"

"Me? No, I—" She was interrupted by her telephone buzzing and could see that Daniel was trying to call her. Again? The buzzing was followed by two chimes: a text message.

Henrik chortled and touched his nose. "I don't like to reveal my sources. But let's just say that Mrs Meyer isn't going to be short of her Raspberry Red almonds for the next few weeks!"

"But what's made Johnny change his tune? He swore blind that it was an accident." Bent looked confused. "Even if I knew that he'd been in the storage hut that morning – and the cigarette ash the police found put him right there at the scene   that didn't mean he'd done anything wrong."

"Apart from leaving his friend to die, you mean?" Kenneth managed to get a word in before refilling his glass.

Bent continued. "But Johnny claimed he fell asleep. That he thought Stig had gone home."

"Oh, right. Like we believe that?"

Henrik - delighted to once again be the main attraction, after an evening that had very much been Bent's – decided it was time to take the floor, front and centre. "Yes, but the evidence they have against Johnny is overwhelming. The hammer he used to kill Stig had been wiped clean of fingerprints, we already knew that. But they found his DNA under Stig's nails. Just like on the telly. My God, but they must have had quite a tumble before he finally threw Stig into the water. Karsten said he should have suspected something when Johnny turned up here early the next day, all scrubbed up and smelling of roses. Johnny had even taken care of Stig's work before Karsten asked him. Because, of course, Johnny knew full well that Stig was…" Henrik shivered and looked down. "Poor Stig. God rest his soul."

Kenneth swigged. "Amen to that! And *skål!*"

Lea continued to look at her phone, her face changing colour by the second. Have dinner with a policeman? An exceptionally good looking policeman. Daniel was new to Strandvig and was probably just looking for company. It would be rude not to, wouldn't it? And why shouldn't she? It wasn't as if Mads—

"Lea Mus, are you with us?"

She forced herself back to the conversation at hand. "What? Yes. But why kill Stig? I mean, what would Johnny get out of it? And how on earth did he think he would get away with it?"

Kenneth piped up. "Johnny must have overheard me giving Stig money for Henrik's surprise party. He wanted in on the job. You know what he was like – would do anything for money."

Henrik tried to reel the story back to himself. "That's where what Johnny said was partly true. He didn't plan to kill him, he asked Stig to meet him down at the club. Was going to ask him for a loan – he had spied Kenneth giving all that money to Stig."

Lea nodded. "I did hear the side door open when I was in the toilets that night, though I didn't see anyone come in. That must have been Johnny?"

Bent sipped his pint. "And that was the wad of money that later mysteriously appeared in Gustav's rucksack."

Lea still didn't understand. "But why did they meet at the Vikings? Didn't Stig think it was fishy? And how on earth did they get in?"

Kenneth continued. "Well they had known each other for years and you know Stig – he would always help you out. So Johnny took Stig's bunch of keys, the set hanging behind the bar here, and got Stig to meet him there. They locked themselves in to the club and sat in the storage hut, just like when they were boys. He said they started drinking – pretty heavily."

"But Stig didn't drink spirits!"

"I know that, Bent. And you know that. But that's what Johnny told the police first of all. And then, of course, the police knew he was lying about that too, because they had the contents of Stig's stomach analysed."

Kenneth groaned and took a swig of Amarone to get rid of squeamish thoughts.

Bent looked hopeful. "No spirits?"

"They don't know exactly what he'd been drinking, but it only amounted to a beer. Maximum two. So he didn't fall in the water by accident."

"I knew it!"

Lea squeezed Bent's hand. "But, Henrik, I still don't understand why Johnny did it?"

"This is where it gets bizarre. He mentioned to Stig that he was thinking of asking Karin out—"

"But there's no way Karin would go out with Johnny. Not with Stig still around—"

"Bent, if you'd let me finish! Yes, to us it was a daft idea. It's like me and Kenneth—" He looked over adoringly at his partner, whose glass was currently empty, but whose eyes were very much full of tears. "Stig and Karin were made for each other. No doubt about that. But Johnny couldn't accept – or maybe didn't want to accept – that Karin would always belong to Stig. They never did get

183

divorced, did they? Johnny reckoned that as Stig 'didn't want her', then he should be able to 'have a shot'."

Bent raised his eyebrows and wrinkled his nose.

"Johnny's words, not mine, Bent. And we all know that Stig was a very easy going guy but – and again, this is according to Johnny's version of events – when Johnny mentioned that he was going to ask Karin out on a date, Stig went berserk. Started shouting, said Johnny wasn't good enough for her. Karin deserved better. Went on and on, and warned Johnny to stay well away from her."

Lea winced. "I always thought Johnny was okay. But on the other hand, he wasn't exactly prime boyfriend material."

Kenneth was ready to join in again, between glasses. "Oh, and who do you think is boyfriend material, Lea? Would that be Mads or, your new friend, Command—"

Henrik looked sweetly at Kenneth. "*Skat*, do you think I can finish, please?"

"Sorry, *skat*! But love does seem to be in the air! Look, here comes Mads now!"

A smiling Mads had just arrived, followed by Daniel, deep in conversation with Karin.

"Ooo, Lea! Daniel is here too. The plot thickens!"

Lea refused to look round and instead, concentrated on looking daggers at Kenneth. Why did everyone have an opinion on her love life?

Henrik sighed and moved around in his chair. "Okay, I'll try and finish quickly—"

"Is that what he said last night, Kenneth?

"Lea Jensen! Naughty girl!" Kenneth held on to his glass to steady himself.

Lea smiled triumphantly at Kenneth – it felt good to be the one setting the cat amongst the pigeons for once. No cupcakes tonight. So there!

Henrik coughed. "So where did we get to? Oh, yes. Stig and Johnny argued. Johnny was angry that Stig didn't want to live with

184

Karin, but no-one else was allowed a chance. Called him a 'goody two shoes' and that Stig had always had it easier than himself."

Now it was Bent's turn to interrupt again. "Stig didn't have it easier. He made better choices."

"Of course he did, Bent. You know that. I know that. We all know that. But Johnny didn't see it that way. He felt like he was the victim. And then he apparently lost control, grabbed the hammer and we know the rest…"

Bent looked down into his glass and sighed. "*Tja.*"

Henrik continued. "Johnny left the empty bottle of *Gammel Dansk* on the deck, in the hope that it would look like an accident. That Stig had been drunk and fallen in. But when he heard the police were investigating, and suspected foul play, he tried shifting the blame on to Mads."

"So I was right that it was Johnny who made that anonymous call to the police? Because he was jealous of Mads having a drink with Karin?"

"Yes, Lea. But the plan backfired, and he panicked. He put Stig's bunch of keys back on the hook behind the bar, and put the bundle of money he'd taken from Stig and planted it in young Gustav's rucksack. Anything to muddy the waters and keep the police off his tail."

"Make no bones about it, Johnny was a coward. And a right bloody idiot."

"Who's a bloody idiot, Bent?" Mads had come over from the bar to join them.

Lea held up her head and looked straight at him. "I can think of quite a few people in Strandvig who fit that description, Mads."

"Uh huh?" He held her gaze just as firmly and took his hand from behind his back. A small, paper wrapped package, complete with a pale pink satin ribbon: a hand-tied bouquet from the florist, not a bunch from the forecourt.

"Lea, these are for you."

# CHAPTER 58

L isbeth swigged back what was left in her crystal glass. "Karsten, another one, please."

Mads and Karin exchanged looks. They had never seen Lisbeth drink, let alone two in a row. And never with such speed.

Even Karsten was puzzled. "Are you sure, my love? Don't want it going to that pretty little Aarhus head—"

Lisbeth's eyes, though still slightly red from another outburst of crying in the car on the return from the Vikings, flashed. "Now, please, Karsten!"

"Whatever you say, my love!"

Lisbeth hopped down off the bar stool, warmth suddenly returning to her feet. She pulled herself up to her full height – which wasn't much above bar height – and turned, a little unsteadily, to address the room. Unfortunately, she was all too easy to miss in the noisy throng.

She went behind the bar, reached behind Karsten and took down the little metal gong and hammer that hung on the wall.

"What are you going to do with that, my love?"

"You'll see!"

Lisbeth pulled out a chair from a table and climbed on to it. And beat the gong for all she was worth. There was silence for a second, then whoops and wolf whistles as the crowd realised what was going on. It had been an excellent night so far, what with Bent's little show, and the entertainment looked set to continue.

"Karsten, get in a round of drinks for everyone here."

Karsten gulped and took a visible step backwards. "What, my love?!"

"You heard what I said. Do it!"

Karsten looked on in shock. What had got in to his meek little mouse from Aarhus?

Lisbeth continued her address to the nation. "Ladies and gentlemen of Strandvig! Regulars and guests. This last round tonight is on us. Strandvig has lost a very special man—" At this she wobbled slightly, but managed to regain control of her balance and composure. "And Strandhøj has lost a very special friend. May he rest in peace."

Mads came over with a glass, brimming with *kirsebærvin* and put a steadying hand on her back. She smiled and held her shaking hand up high. "Here's to Stig!"

"To Stig!"

"To Stig!"

Lisbeth took a good look around the room, full of friendly faces, and downed her glass in one. "*Skål!*"

Mads gently caught her as she collapsed.

CHAPTER 59

K arsten closed the till and looked around the room with a satisfying smile. Then cranked up the volume and started singing along with John Mogensen.

*"Life is short, life is short, think very carefully before you throw it away…"*

Lea put down her wine glass and looked at her watch. "Is it that time already? I should make a move. It's been an extremely long day and I need a very long, and very hot, shower."

"Goodnight, Lea Mus." Bent put one hand on the bar to steady himself and turned around on his bar stool. "Straight home tonight?"

Lea stopped searching in her handbag, looked up at him and raised her eyebrows.

"Okay, Lea Mus. But are you quite sure you don't want me to cycle with you? I don't mind."

Lea looked at him and laughed. "Not this again, please, Bent! I'm a big girl. Remember?"

"Sorry, Lea Mus. Old habits, you know…"

"And this from the man who got himself stuck in a storage hut—"

"Point taken! I won't mention it again. *Ama'r halshug!*"

Lea gave Bent a squeeze and a peck on the cheek, wrapped her scarf around her neck three times and walked out the side door towards the car park, carrying herself a little taller than she normally did. The small bouquet of flowers sticking out from the top of her handbag.

Bent turned back around and started on his final half pint of the evening. Then watched, intrigued, as Mads and Daniel both hurriedly put on their jackets and headed out after Lea, almost colliding with each other in the doorway to the car park. Bent put down his glass and scratched his head. "What do you reckon is going on there, Karsten?"

Karsten stopped polishing glasses and looked over towards the door. "Between you and me, Bent, I don't really think they quite know themselves."

He picked up another glass and winked at Bent. "But my money's on Mads."

"My money's on Daniel. *Skål!*"

"*Skål!*"

Karsten put down his dishtowel and leaned in. "Bent, did you hear about the man from Aarhus who—"

Made in the USA
Las Vegas, NV
27 January 2022

42407272R00108